WILLIAM GOLDING

Pincher Martin

With an afterword by Philippa Gregory

D1332081

ff

faber and faber

First published in 1956
by Faber and Faber Limited
Bloomsbury House, 77-77 Great Russell Street, London wc1b 3da
This paperback edition first published in 2013

Printed and bound by CPI Group (UK) Ltd, Croydon, cr0 4yy

All rights reserved

© William Golding, 1956
Afterword © Philippa Gregory, 2013

William Golding is hereby identified as author of this work in accordance with
Section 77 of the Copyright, Designs and Patents Act 1988

*This book is sold subject to the condition that it shall not, by way of trade or otherwise,
be lent, resold, hired out or otherwise circulated without the publisher's prior consent in
any form of binding or cover other than that in which it is published and without a
similar condition including this condition being imposed on the subsequent purchaser*

A CIP record for this book is available from the British Library

isbn 978-0-571-29850-1

HEREFORDSHIRE LIBRARIES	
020	
Bertrams	30/08/2013
GEN	£8.99
HC	

2 4 6 8 10 9 7 5 3 1

1

He was struggling in every direction, he was the centre of the writhing and kicking knot of his own body. There was no up or down, no light and no air. He felt his mouth open of itself and the shrieked word burst out.

"Help!"

When the air had gone with the shriek, water came in to fill its place—burning water, hard in the throat and mouth as stones that hurt. He hutched his body towards the place where air had been but now it was gone and there was nothing but black, choking welter. His body let loose its panic and his mouth strained open till the hinges of his jaw hurt. Water thrust in, down, without mercy. Air came with it for a moment so that he fought in what might have been the right direction. But water reclaimed him and spun so that knowledge of where the air might be was erased completely. Turbines were screaming in his ears and green sparks flew out from the centre like tracer. There was a piston engine too, racing out of gear and making the whole universe shake. Then for a moment there was air like a cold mask against his face and he bit into it. Air and water mixed, dragged down into his body like gravel. Muscles, nerves and blood, struggling lungs, a machine in the head, they worked for one moment in an ancient pattern. The lumps of hard water jerked in the gullet, the lips came together and parted, the tongue arched, the brain lit a neon track.

"Moth——"

But the man lay suspended behind the whole commotion, detached from his jerking body. The luminous pictures that were shuffled before him were drenched in light but he paid no attention to them. Could he have controlled the nerves of his face, or could a face have been fashioned to fit the attitude of his consciousness where it lay suspended between life and death that face would have worn a snarl. But the real jaw was contorted down and distant, the mouth was slopped full. The green tracer that flew from the centre began to spin into a disc. The throat at such a distance from the snarling man vomited water and drew it in again. The hard lumps of water no longer hurt. There was a kind of truce, observation of the body. There was no face but there was a snarl.

A picture steadied and the man regarded it. He had not seen such a thing for so many years that the snarl became curious and lost a little intensity. It examined the picture.

The jam jar was standing on a table, brightly lit from O.P. It might have been a huge jar in the centre of a stage or a small one almost touching the face, but it was interesting because one could see into a little world there which was quite separate but which one could control.

2

The jar was nearly full of clear water and a tiny glass figure floated upright in it. The top of the jar was covered with a thin membrane—white rubber. He watched the jar without moving or thinking while his distant body stilled itself and relaxed. The pleasure of the jar lay in the fact that the little glass figure was so delicately balanced between opposing forces. Lay a finger on the membrane and you would compress the air below it which in turn would press more strongly on the water. Then the water would force itself farther up the little tube in the figure, and it would begin to sink. By varying the pressure on the membrane you could do anything you liked with the glass figure which was wholly in your power. You could mutter,—sink now! And down it would go, down, down; you could steady it and relent. You could let it struggle towards the surface, give it almost a bit of air then send it steadily, slowly, remorselessly down and down.

The delicate balance of the glass figure related itself to his body. In a moment of wordless realization he saw himself touching the surface of the sea with just such a dangerous stability, poised between floating and going down. The snarl thought words to itself. They were not articulate, but they were there in a luminous way as a realization.

Of course. My lifebelt.

It was bound by the tapes under that arm and that. The tapes went over the shoulders—and now he could even feel them—went round the chest and were fastened in front under the oilskin and duffle. It was almost deflated

3

as recommended by the authorities because a tightly blown-up belt might burst when you hit the water. Swim away from the ship then blow up your belt.

With the realization of the lifebelt a flood of connected images came back—the varnished board on which the instructions were displayed, pictures of the lifebelt itself with the tube and metal tit threaded through the tapes. Suddenly he knew who he was and where he was. He was lying suspended in the water like the glass figure; he was not struggling but limp. A swell was washing regularly over his head.

His mouth slopped full and he choked. Flashes of tracer cut the darkness. He felt a weight pulling him down. The snarl came back with a picture of heavy seaboots and he began to move his legs. He got one toe over the other and shoved but the boot would not come off. He gathered himself and there were his hands far off but serviceable. He shut his mouth and performed a grim acrobatic in the water while the tracer flashed. He felt his heart thumping and for a while it was the only point of reference in the formless darkness. He got his right leg across his left thigh and heaved with sodden hands. The seaboot slipped down his calf and he kicked it free. Once the rubber top had left his toes he felt it touch him once and then it was gone utterly. He forced his left leg up, wrestled with the second boot and got it free. Both boots had left him. He let his body uncoil and lie limply.

His mouth was clever. It opened and shut for the air

and against the water. His body understood too. Every now and then it would clench its stomach into a hard knot and sea water would burst out over his tongue. He began to be frightened again—not with animal panic but with deep fear of death in isolation and long drawn out. The snarl came back but now it had a face to use and air for the throat. There was something meaningful behind the snarl which would not waste the air on noises. There was a purpose which had not yet had time and experience to discover how relentless it was. It could not use the mechanism for regular breathing but it took air in gulps between the moments of burial.

He began to think in gulps as he swallowed the air. He remembered his hands again and there they were in the darkness, far away. He brought them in and began to fumble at the hard stuff of his oilskin. The button hurt and would hardly be persuaded to go through the hole. He slipped the loop off the toggle of his duffle. Lying with little movement of his body he found that the sea ignored him, treated him as a glass figure of a sailor or as a log that was almost ready to sink but would last a few moments yet. The air was regularly in attendance between the passage of the swells.

He got the rubber tube and drew it through the tapes. He could feel the slack and uninflated rubber that was so nearly not holding him up. He got the tit of the tube between his teeth and unscrewed with two fingers while the others sealed the tube. He won a little air from

5

between swells and fuffed it through the rubber tube. For uncounted numbers of swell and hollow he taxed the air that might have gone into his lungs until his heart was staggering in his body like a wounded man and the green tracer was flicking and spinning. The lifebelt began to firm up against his chest but so slowly that he could not tell when the change came. Then abruptly the swells were washing over his shoulders and the repeated burial beneath them had become a wet and splashing slap in the face. He found he had no need to play catch-as-catch-can for air. He blew deeply and regularly into the tube until the lifebelt rose and strained at his clothing. Yet he did not stop blowing at once. He played with the air, letting a little out and then blowing again as if frightened of stopping the one positive action he could take to help himself. His head and neck and shoulders were out of the water now for long intervals. They were colder than the rest of his body. The air stiffened them. They began to shake.

He took his mouth from the tube.

"Help! Help!"

The air escaped from the tube and he struggled with it. He twisted the tit until the air was safe. He stopped shouting and strained his eyes to see through the darkness but it lay right against his eyeballs. He put his hand before his eyes and saw nothing. Immediately the terror of blindness added itself to the terror of isolation and drowning. He began to make vague climbing motions in the water.

"Help! Is there anybody there? Help! Survivor!"

He lay shaking for a while and listened for an answer but the only sound was the hissing and puddling of the water as it washed round him. His head fell forward.

He licked salt water off his lips.

"Exercise."

He began to tread water gently. His mouth mumbled.

"Why did I take my sea boots off? I'm no better off than I was." His head nodded forward again.

"Cold. Mustn't get too cold. If I had those boots I could put them on and then take them off and then put them on——"

He thought suddenly of the boat sinking through water towards a bottom that was still perhaps a mile remote from them. With that, the whole wet immensity seemed to squeeze his body as though he were sunk to a great depth. His chattering teeth came together and the flesh of his face twisted. He arched in the water, drawing his feet up away from the depth, the slopping, glutinous welter.

"Help! Help——"

He began to thresh with his hands and force his body round. He stared at the darkness as he turned but there was nothing to tell him when he had completed the circle and everywhere the darkness was grainless and alike. There was no wreckage, no sinking hull, no struggling survivors but himself, there was only darkness lying close against the balls of the eyes. There was the movement of water.

He began to cry out for the others, for anyone.

"Nat! Nathaniel! For Christ's sake! Nathaniel! Help!"

His voice died and his face untwisted. He lay slackly in his lifebelt, allowing the swell to do what it would. His teeth were chattering again and sometimes this vibration would spread till it included his whole body. His legs below him were not cold so much as pressed, squeezed mercilessly by the sea so that the feeling in them was not a response to temperature but to weight that would crush and burst them. He searched for a place to put his hands but there was nowhere that kept the ache out of them. The back of his neck began to hurt and that not gradually but with a sudden stab of pain so that holding his chin away from his chest was impossible. But this put his face into the sea so that he sucked it into his nose with a snoring noise and a choke. He spat and endured the pain in his neck for a while. He wedged his hands between his lifebelt and his chin and for a swell or two this was some relief but then the pain returned. He let his hands fall away and his face dipped in the water. He lay back, forcing his head against the pain so that his eyes if they had been open would have been looking at the sky. The pressure on his legs was bearable now. They were no longer flesh, but had been transformed to some other substance, petrified and comfortable. The part of his body that had not been invaded and wholly subdued by the sea was jerking intermittently. Eternity, inseparable from pain was there to be examined and experienced. The snarl endured. He thought. The thoughts were laborious, disconnected but vital.

8

Presently it will be daylight.

I must move from one point to another.

Enough to see one move ahead.

Presently it will be daylight.

I shall see wreckage.

I won't die.

I can't die.

Not me——

Precious.

He roused himself with a sudden surge of feeling that had nothing to do with the touch of the sea. Salt water was coming fast out of his eyes. He snivelled and gulped.

"Help, somebody—help!"

His body lifted and fell gently.

If I'd been below I might have got to a boat even. Or a raft. But it had to be my bloody watch. Blown off the bloody bridge. She must have gone on perhaps to starboard if he got the order in time, sinking or turning over. They'll be there in the darkness somewhere where she sank asking each other if they're down-hearted, knots and stipples of heads in the water and oil and drifting stuff. When it's light I must find them, Christ I must find them. Or they'll be picked up and I'll be left to swell like a hammock. Christ!

"Help! Nathaniel! Help——!"

And I gave the right orders too. If I'd done it ten seconds earlier I'd be a bloody hero—Hard a-starboard for Christ's sake!

Must have hit us bang under the bridge. And I gave the right order. And I get blown to buggery.

The snarl fixed itself, worked on the wooden face till the upper lip was lifted and the chattering teeth bared. The little warmth of anger flushed blood back into the tops of the cheeks and behind the eyes. They opened.

Then he was jerking and splashing and looking up. There was a difference in the texture of the darkness; there were smears and patches that were not in the eye itself. For a moment and before he remembered how to use his sight the patches lay on the eyeballs as close as the darkness had been. Then he firmed the use of his eyes and he was inside his head, looking out through the arches of his skull at random formations of dim light and mist. However he blinked and squinted they remained there outside him. He bent his head forward and saw, fainter than an afterimage, the scalloped and changing shape of a swell as his body was lifted in it. For a moment he caught the inconstant outline against the sky, then he was floating up and seeing dimly the black top of the next swell as it swept towards him. He began to make swimming motions. His hands were glimmering patches in the water and his movements broke up the stony weight of his legs. The thoughts continued to flicker.

We were travelling north-east. I gave the order. If he began the turn she might be anywhere over there to the east. The wind was westerly. That's the east over there where the swells are running away down hill.

His movements and his breathing became fierce. He swam a sort of clumsy breast-stroke, buoyed up on the inflated belt. He stopped and lay wallowing. He set his teeth, took the tit of the lifebelt and let out air till he was lying lower in the water. He began to swim again. His breathing laboured. He stared out of his arches intently and painfully at the back of each swell as it slunk away from him. His legs slowed and stopped; his arms fell. His mind inside the dark skull made swimming movements long after the body lay motionless in the water.

The grain of the sky was more distinct. There were vaporous changes of tone from dark to gloom, to grey. Near at hand the individual hillocks of the surface were visible. His mind made swimming movements.

Pictures invaded his mind and tried to get between him and the urgency of his motion towards the east. The jam jar came back but robbed of significance. There was a man, a brief interview, a desk-top so polished that the smile of teeth was being reflected in it. There was a row of huge masks hung up to dry and a voice from behind the teeth that had been reflected in the desk spoke softly.

"Which one do you think would suit Christopher?"

There was a binnacle-top with the compass light just visible, there was an order shouted, hung up there for all heaven and earth to see in neon lighting.

"Hard a-starboard, for Christ's sake!"

Water washed into his mouth and he jerked into consciousness with a sound that was half a snore and half a choke. The day was inexorably present in green and grey. The seas were intimate and enormous. They smoked. When he swung up a broad, hilly crest he could see two other smoking crests then nothing but a vague circle that might be mist or fine spray or rain. He peered into the circle, turning himself, judging direction by the run of the water until he had inspected every part. The slow fire of his belly, banked up to endure, was invaded. It lay defenceless in the middle of the clothing and sodden body.

"I won't die! I won't!"

The circle of mist was everywhere alike. Crests swung into view on that side, loomed, seized him, elevated him for a moment, let him down and slunk off, but there was another crest to take him, lift him so that he could see the last one just dimming out of the circle. Then he would go down again and another crest would loom weltering towards him.

He began to curse and beat the water with the flat of his white hands. He struggled up the swells. But even the sounds of his working mouth and body were merged unnoticed in the innumerable sounds of travelling water. He hung still in his belt, feeling the cold search his belly with its fingers. His head fell on his chest and the stuff slopped weakly, peristently over his face. Think. My last chance. Think what can be done.

She sank out in the Atlantic. Hundreds of miles from land. She was alone, sent north-east from the convoy to break WT silence. The U-boat may be hanging round to pick up a survivor or two for questioning. Or to pick off any ship that comes to rescue survivors. She may surface at any moment, breaking the swell with her heavy body like a half-tide rock. Her periscope may sear the water close by, eye of a land-creature that has defeated the rhythm and necessity of the sea. She may be passing under me now, shadowy and shark-like, she may be lying down there below my wooden feet on a bed of salty water as on a cushion while her crew sleeps. Survivors, a raft, the whaler, the dinghy, wreckage may be milling about only a swell or two away hidden in the mist and waiting for rescue with at least bully and perhaps a tot.

He began to rotate in the water again, peering blearily at the midst, he squinted at the sky that was not much higher than a roof; he searched the circle for wreckage or a head. But there was nothing. She had gone as if a hand had reached up that vertical mile and snatched her down in one motion. When he thought of the mile he arched in the water, face twisted, and began to cry out.

"Help, curse you, sod you, bugger you—Help!"

Then he was blubbering and shuddering and the cold was squeezing him like the hand that had snatched down the ship. He hiccupped slowly into silence and started to rotate once more in the smoke and green welter.

One side of the circle was lighter than the other. The swell was shouldering itself on towards the left of this vague brightness; and where the brightness spread the mist was even more impenetrable than behind him. He remained facing the brightness not because it was of any use to him but because it was a difference that broke the uniformity of the circle and because it looked a little warmer than anywhere else. He made swimming movements again without thought and as if to follow in the wake of that brightness was an inevitable thing to do. The light made the sea-smoke seem solid. It penetrated the water so that between him and the very tops of the restless hillocks it was bottle green. For a moment or two after a wave had passed he could see right into it but the waves were nothing but water—there was no weed in them, no speck of solid, nothing drifting, nothing moving but green water, cold persistent idiot water. There were hands to be sure and two forearms of black oilskin and there was the noise of breathing, gasping. There was also the noise of the idiot stuff, whispering, folding on itself, tripped ripples running tinkling by the ear like miniatures of surf on a flat beach; there were sudden hisses and spats, roars and incompleted syllables and the soft friction of wind. The hands were important under the bright side of the circle but they had nothing to seize on. There was an infinite drop of the soft, cold stuff below them and under the labouring, dying, body.

The sense of depth caught him and he drew his dead feet up to his belly as if to detach them from the whole ocean. He arched and gaped, he rose over the chasm of deep sea on a swell and his mouth opened to scream against the brightness.

14

It stayed open. Then it shut with a snap of teeth and his arms began to heave water out of the way. He fought his way forward.

"Ahoy—for Christ's sake! Survivor! Survivor! Fine on your starboard bow!"

He threshed with his arms and legs into a clumsy crawl. A crest overtook him and he jerked himself to the chest out of water.

"Help! Help! Survivor! For God's sake!"

The force of his return sent him under but he struggled up and shook the wave from his head. The fire of his belly had spread and his heart was thrusting the sluggish blood painfully round his body. There was a ship in the mist to port of the bright patch. He was on her starboard bow—or—and the thought drove him to foam in the water—he was on her port quarter and she was moving away. But even in his fury of movement he saw how impossible this was since then she would have passed by him only a few minutes ago. So she was coming towards, to cut across the circle of visibility only a few yards from him.

Or stopped.

At that, he stopped too, and lay in the water. She was so dull a shape, little more than a looming darkness that he could not tell both her distance and her size. She was more nearly bows on than when he had first seen her and now she was visible even when he was in a trough. He began to swim again but every time he rose on a crest he screamed.

"Help! Survivor!"

15

But what ship was ever so lop-sided? A carrier? A derelict carrier, deserted and waiting to sink? But she would have been knocked down by a salvo of torpedoes. A derelict liner? Then she must be one of the Queens by her bulk—and why lop-sided? The sun and the mist were balanced against each other. The sun could illumine the mist but not pierce it. And darkly in the sun-mist loomed the shape of a not-ship where nothing but a ship could be.

He began to swim again, feeling suddenly the desperate exhaustion of his body. The first, fierce excitement of sighting had burned up the fuel and the fire was low again. He swam grimly, forcing his arms through the water, reaching forward under his arches with sight as though he could pull himself into safety with it. The shape moved. It grew larger and not clearer. Every now and then there was something like a bow-wave at the forefoot. He ceased to look at her but swam and screamed alternately with the last strength of his body. There was green force round him, growing in strength to rob, there was mist and glitter over him; there was a redness pulsing in front of his eyes—his body gave up and he lay slack in the waves and the shape rose over him. He heard through the rasp and thump of his works the sound of waves breaking. He lifted his head and there was rock stuck up in the sky with a sea-gull poised before it. He heaved over in the sea and saw how each swell dipped for a moment, flung up a white hand of foam then disappeared as if the rock had swallowed it. He began to think swimming motions but knew

16

now that his body was no longer obedient. The top of
the next swell between him and the rock was blunted,
smoothed curiously, then jerked up spray. He sank down,
saw without comprehension that the green water was no
longer empty. There was yellow and brown. He heard not
the formless mad talking of uncontrolled water but a sudden roar. Then he went under into a singing world and
there were hairy shapes that flitted and twisted past his
face, there were sudden notable details close to of intricate rock and weed. Brown tendrils slashed across his face,
then with a destroying shock he hit solidity. It was utter
difference, it was under his body, against his knees and
face, he could close fingers on it, for an instance he could
even hold on. His mouth was needlessly open and his eyes
so that he had a moment of close and intent communion
with three limpets, two small and one large that were only
an inch or two from his face. Yet this solidity was terrible
and apocalyptic after the world of inconstant wetness. It
was not vibrant as a ship's hull might be but merciless
and mother of panic. It had no business to interrupt the
thousands of miles of water going about their purposeless
affairs and therefore the world sprang here into sudden
war. He felt himself picked up and away from the limpets,
reversed, tugged, thrust down into weed and darkness.
Ropes held him, slipped and let him go. He saw light, got
a mouthful of air and foam. He glimpsed a riven rock face
with trees of spray growing up it and the sight of this rock
floating in mid-Atlantic was so dreadful that he wasted his

17

air by screaming as if it had been a wild beast. He went under into a green calm, then up and was thrust sideways. The sea no longer played with him. It stayed its wild movement and held him gently, carried him with delicate and careful motion like a retriever with a bird. Hard things touched him about the feet and knees. The sea laid him down gently and retreated. There were hard things touching his face and chest, the side of his forehead. The sea came back and fawned round his face, licked him. He thought movements that did not happen. The sea came back and he thought the movements again and this time they happened because the sea took most of his weight. They moved him forward over the hard things. Each wave and each movement moved him forward. He felt the sea run down to smell at his feet then come back and nuzzle under his arm. It no longer licked his face. There was a pattern in front of him that occupied all the space under the arches. It meant nothing. The sea nuzzled under his arm again.

He lay still.

2

The pattern was white and black but mostly white. It existed in two layers, one behind the other, one for each eye. He thought nothing, did nothing while the pattern changed a trifle and made little noises. The hardnesses under his cheek began to insist. They passed through pressure to a burning without heat, to a localized pain. They became vicious in their insistence like the nag of an aching tooth. They began to pull him back into himself and organize him again as a single being.

Yet it was not the pain nor the white and black pattern that first brought him back to life, but the noises. Though the sea had treated him so carefully, elsewhere it continued to roar and thump and collapse on itself. The wind too, given something to fight with other than obsequious water was hissing round the rock and breathing gustily in crevices. All these noises made a language which forced itself into the dark, passionless head and assured it that the head was somewhere, somewhere—and then finally with the flourish of a gull's cry over the sound of wind and water, declared to the groping consciousness: wherever you are, you are here!

Then he was there, suddenly, enduring pain but in deep communion with the solidity that held up his body. He remembered how eyes should be used and brought the two lines of sight together so that the patterns fused and made a distance. The pebbles were close to his face, pressing against his cheek and jaw. They were white quartz, dulled and rounded, a miscellany of potato-shapes. Their whiteness was qualified by yellow stains and flecks of darker material. There was a whiter thing beyond them. He examined it without curiosity, noting the bleached wrinkles, the blue roots of nails, the corrugations at the finger-tips. He did not move his head but followed the line of the hand back to an oil-skin sleeve, the beginnings of a shoulder. His eyes returned to the pebbles and watched them idly as if they were about to perform some operation for which he was waiting without much interest. The hand did not move.

Water welled up among the pebbles. It stirred them slightly, paused, then sank away while the pebbles clicked and chirruped. It swilled down past his body and pulled gently at his stockinged feet. He watched the pebbles while the water came back and this time the last touch of the sea lopped into his open mouth. Without change of expression he began to shake, a deep shake that included the whole of his body. Inside his head it seemed that the pebbles were shaking because the movement of his white hand forward and back was matched by the movement of his body. Under the side of his face the pebbles nagged.

The pictures that came and went inside his head did

not disturb him because they were so small and remote. There was a woman's body, white and detailed, there was a boy's body; there was a box office, the bridge of a ship, an order picked out across a far sky in neon lighting, a tall, thin man who stood aside humbly in the darkness at the top of a companion ladder; there was a man hanging in the sea like a glass sailor in a jam jar. There was nothing to choose between the pebbles and pictures. Sometimes one was uppermost, sometimes the other. The individual pebbles were no bigger than the pictures. Sometimes a pebble would be occupied entirely by a picture as though it were a window, a spy-hole into a different world or other dimension. Words and sounds were sometimes visible as shapes like the shouted order. They did not vibrate and disappear. When they were created they remained as hard enduring things like the pebbles. Some of these were inside the skull, behind the arch of the brow and the shadowy nose. They were right in the indeterminate darkness above the fire of hardnesses. If you looked out idly, you saw round them.

There was a new kind of coldness over his body. It was creeping down his back between the stuffed layers of clothing. It was air that felt like slow fire. He had hardly noticed this when a wave came back and filled his mouth so that a choke interrupted the rhythm of shaking.

He began to experiment. He found that he could haul the weight of one leg up and then the other. His hand crawled round above his head. He reasoned deeply that

21

there was another hand on the other side somewhere and sent a message out to it. He found the hand and worked the wrist. There were still fingers on it, not because he could move them but because when he pushed he could feel the wooden tips shifting the invisible pebbles. He moved his four limbs in close and began to make swimming movements. The vibrations from the cold helped him. Now his breath went in and out quickly and his heart began to race again. The inconsequential pictures vanished and there was nothing but pebbles and pebble noises and heart-thumps. He had a valuable thought, not because it was of immediate physical value but because it gave him back a bit of his personality. He made words to express this thought, though they did not pass the barrier of his teeth.

"I should be about as heavy as this on Jupiter."

At once he was master. He knew that his body weighed no more than it had always done, that it was exhausted, that he was trying to crawl up a little pebble slope. He lifted the dents in his face away from the pebbles that had made them and pushed with his knees. His teeth came together and ground. He timed the expansion of his chest against the pebbles, the slow shaking of his body till they did not hold up the leaden journey. He felt how each wave finished farther and farther down towards his feet. When the journey became too desperate he would wait, gasping, until the world came back. The water no longer touched his feet.

His left hand—the hidden one—touched something that did not click and give. He rolled his head and looked up under the arch. There was greyish yellow stuff in front of his face. It was pock-marked and hollowed, dotted with red lumps of jelly. The yellow tents of limpets were pitched in every hole. Brown fronds and green webs of weed hung over them. The white pebbles led up into a dark angle. There was a film of water glistening over everything, drops falling, tiny pools caught at random, lying and shuddering or leaking down among the weed. He began to turn on the pebbles, working his back against the rock and drawing up his feet. He saw them now for the first time, distant projections, made thick and bear-like by the white, seaboot stockings. They gave him back a little more of himself. He got his left hand down beneath his ear and began to heave. His shoulder lifted a little. He pushed with feet, pulled with hands. His back was edging into the angle where the pools leaked down. His head was high. He took a thigh in both hands and pulled it towards his chest and then the other. He packed himself into the angle and looked down at the pebbles over his knees. His mouth had fallen open again.

And after all, as pebbles go there were not very many of them. The length of a man or less would measure out the sides of the triangle that they made under the shadow of the rock. They filled the cleft and they were solid.

He took his eyes away from the pebbles and made them examine the water. This was almost calm in comparison with the open sea; and the reason was the rock round which the waves had whirled him. He could see the rock out there now. It was the same stuff as this, grey and creamy with barnacles and foam. Each wave tripped on it so that although the water ran and thumped on either side of the cleft, there was a few yards of green, clear water between him and the creamy rock. Beyond the rock was nothing but a smoking advance of sea with watery sunlight caught in it.

He let his eyes close and ignored the pictures that came and went behind them. The slow movement of his mind settled on a thought. There was a small fire in his body that was almost extinguished but incredibly was still smouldering despite the Atlantic. He folded his body consciously round that fire and nursed it. There was not more than a spark. The formal words and the pictures evolved themselves.

A seabird cried over him with a long sound descending down wind. He removed his attention from the spark of fire and opened his eyes again. This time he had got back so much of his personality that he could look out and grasp the whole of what he saw at once. There were the dark walls of rock on either side that framed the brighter light. There was sunlight on a rock with spray round it and the steady march of swells that brought their own fine mist along with them under the sun. He turned his head sideways and peered up.

The rock was smoother above the weeds and limpets

and drew together. There was an opening at the top with daylight and the suggestion of cloud caught in it. As he watched, a gull flicked across the opening and cried in the wind. He found the effort of looking up hurt him and he turned to his body, examined the humps that were his knees under the oilskin and duffle. He looked closely at a button.

His mouth shut then opened. Sounds came out. He re-adjusted them and they were uncertain words.

"I know you. Nathaniel sewed you on. I asked him to. Said it was an excuse to get him away from the mess-deck for a bit of peace."

His eyes closed again and he fingered the button clumsily.

"Had this oilskin when I was a rating. Lofty sewed on the buttons before Nathaniel."

His head nodded on his knees.

"All the blue watch. Blue watch to muster."

The pictures were interrupted by the solid shape of a snore. The shiverings were less dramatic but they took power from his arms so that presently they fell away from his knees and his hands lay on the pebbles. His head shook. Between the snores the pebbles were hard to the feet, harder to the backside when the heels had slid slowly from under. The pictures were so confused that there was as much danger that they would destroy the personality as that the spark of fire would go out. He forced his way among them, lifted his eyelids and looked out.

The pebbles were wavering down there where the water welled over them. Higher up, the rock that had saved him was lathered and fringed with leaping strings of foam. There was afternoon brightness outside but the cleft was dripping, dank and smelly as a dockside latrine. He made quacking sounds with his mouth. The words that had formed in his mind were: Where is this bloody rock? But that seemed to risk something by insult of the dark cleft so that he changed them in his throat.

"Where the hell am I?"

A single point of rock, peak of a mountain range, one tooth set in the ancient jaw of a sunken world, projecting through the inconceivable vastness of the whole ocean—and how many miles from dry land? An evil pervasion, not the convulsive panic of his first struggles in the water, but a deep and generalized terror set him clawing at the rock with his blunt fingers. He even got half-up and leaned or crouched against the weed and the lumps of jelly.

"Think, you bloody fool, think."

The horizon of misty water stayed close, the water leapt from the rock and the pebbles wavered.

"Think."

He crouched, watching the rock, not moving but trembling continually. He noted how the waves broke on the outer rock and were tamed, so that the water before the cleft was sloppily harmless. Slowly, he settled back into the angle of the cleft. The spark was alight and the heart was supplying it with what it wanted. He watched the outer rock but hardly saw it. There was a name missing. That name was written on the chart, well out in the Atlantic, eccentrically isolated so that seamen who could to a certain extent laugh at wind and weather had made a joke of the rock. Frowning, he saw the chart now in his mind's eye but not clearly. He saw the navigating commander of the cruiser bending over it with the captain, saw himself as navigator's yeoman standing ready while they grinned at each other. The captain spoke with his clipped Dartmouth accent—spoke and laughed.

"I call that name a near miss."

Near miss whatever the name was. And now to be huddled on a near miss how many miles from the Hebrides? What was the use of the spark if it winked away in a crack of that ludicrous isolation? He spat his words at the picture of the captain.

"I am no better off than I was."

He began to slide down the rocks as his bones bent their hinges. He slumped into the angle and his head fell. He snored.

But inside, where the snores were external, the consciousness was moving and poking about among the pictures and revelations, among the shape-sounds and the disregarded feelings like an animal ceaselessly examining its cage. It rejected the detailed bodies of women, slowly sorted the odd words, ignored the pains and the insistence of the shaking body. It was looking for a thought. It found the thought, separated it from the junk, lifted it and used the apparatus of the body to give it force and importance.

"I am intelligent."

There was a period of black suspension behind the snores; then the right hand, so far away, obeyed a command and began to fumble and pluck at the oilskin. It raised a flap and crawled inside. The fingers found cord and a shut clasp-knife. They stayed there.

The eyes blinked open so that the arch of brows was a frame to green sea. For a while the eyes looked, received impressions without seeing them. Then the whole body gave a jump. The spark became a flame, the body scrambled, crouched, the hand flicked out of the oilskin pocket and grabbed rock. The eyes stared and did not blink.

As the eyes watched, a wave went clear over the outer rock so that they could see the brown weed inside the water. The green dance beyond the pebbles was troubled. A line of foam broke and hissed up the pebbles to his feet. The foam sank away and the pebbles chattered like teeth. He watched, wave after wave as bursts of foam swallowed more and more of the pebbles and left fewer visible when they went back. The outer rock was no longer a barrier but only a gesture of defence. The cleft was being connected more and more directly with the irrestible progress of the green, smoking seas. He jerked away from the open water and turned towards the rock. The dark, lavatorial cleft, with its dripping weed, with its sessile, mindless life of shell and jelly was land only twice a day by courtesy of the moon. It felt like solidity but it was a sea-trap, as alien to breathing life as the soft slop of the last night and the vertical mile.

A gull screamed with him so that he came back into himself, leaned his forehead against the rock and waited for his heart to steady. A shot of foam went over his feet. He looked down past them. There were fewer pebbles to stand on and those that had met his hands when he had been washed ashore were yellow and green beneath a foot of jumping water. He turned to the rock again and spoke out loud.

"Climb!"

He turned round and found handholds in the cleft. There were many to choose from. His hands were poor, sodden stuff against their wet projections. He leaned a moment against the rock and gathered the resources of his body together. He lifted his right leg and dropped the foot in an opening like an ash-tray. There was an edge to the ash-tray but not a sharp one and his foot could feel nothing. He took his forehead away from a weedy surface and heaved himself up until the right leg was straight. His left leg swung and thumped. He got the toes on a shelf and stayed so, only a few inches off the pebbles and spreadeagled. The cleft rose by his face and he looked at the secret drops of the stillicide in the dark angle as though he envied them their peace. Time went by drop by drop. The two pictures drifted apart.

The pebbles rattled below him and a last lick of water flipped into the crevice. He dropped his head and looked down over his lifebelt, through the open skirt of the oilskin to where the wetted pebbles lay in the angle of the cleft. He saw his seaboot stockings and thought his feet back into them.

"I wish I had my seaboots still."

He changed the position of his right foot cautiously and locked his left knee stiffly upright to bear his weight without effort. His feet were selective in a curious way. They could not feel rock unless there was sharpness. They only became a part of him when they were hurting him or when he could see them.

The tail end of a wave reached right into the angle and struck in the apex with a plop. A single string of spray leapt up between his legs, past the lifebelt and wetted his face. He made a sound and only then found how ruinous an extension of flesh he carried round him. The sound began in the throat, bubbled and stayed there. The mouth took no part but lay open, jaw lying slack on the hard oilskin collar. The bubbling increased and he made the teeth click. Words twisted out between them and the frozen stuff of his upper lip.

"Like a dead man!"

Another wave reached in and spray ran down his face. He began to labour at climbing. He moved up the intricate rock face until there were no more limpets nor mussels and nothing clung to the rock but his own body and tiny

30

barnacles and green smears of weed. All the time the wind pushed him into the cleft and the sea made dispersed noises.

The cleft narrowed until his head projected through an opening, not much wider than his body. He got his elbows jammed on either side and looked up.

Before his face the rock widened above the narrowest part of the cleft into a funnel. The sides of the funnel were not very smooth; but they were smooth enough to refuse to hold a body by friction. They sloped away to the top of the rock like a roof angle. The track from his face to the cliff-like edge of the funnel at the top was nearly twice the length of a man. He began to turn his head, slowly, searching for handholds, but saw none. Only at about halfway there was a depression, but too shallow for a handhold. Blunted fingers would never be safe on the rounded edge.

There came a thud from the bottom of the angle. Solid water shot into the angle, burst and washed down again. He peered over his lifebelt, between his two feet. The pebbles were dimmed, appeared clearly for a moment, then vanished under a surge of green water. Spray shot up between his body and the rock.

He pulled himself up until his body from the waist was leaning forward along the slope. His feet found the holds where his elbows had been. His knees straightened slowly while he breathed in gasps and his right arm reached out in front of him. Fingers closed on the blunted edge of the depression. Pulled.

31

He took one foot away from a hold and edged the knee up. He moved the other.

He hung, only a few inches from the top of the angle, held by one hand and the friction of his body. The fingers of his right hand quivered and gave. They slipped over the rounded edge. His whole body slid down and he was back at the top of the crevice again. He lay still, not seeing the rock by his eyes and his right arm was stretched above him.

The sea was taking over the cleft. Every few seconds there came the thump and return of a wave below him. Heavy drops fell and trickled on the surface of the funnel before his face. Then a wave exploded and water cascaded over his legs. He lifted his face off the rock and the snarl wrestled with his stiff muscles.

"Like a limpet."

He lay for a while, bent at the top of the crevice. The pebbles no longer appeared in the angle. They were a wavering memory of themselves between bouts of spray. Then they vanished, the rock vanished with them and with another explosion the water hit him from head to foot. He shook it from his face. He was staring down at the crevice as though the water were irrelevant.

He cried out.

"Like a limpet!"

He put his feet down and felt for holds, lowered himself resolutely, clinging each time the water hit him and went back. He held his breath and spat when each wave left him. The water was no longer cold but powerful rather. The nearer he lowered his body to the pebbles the harder he was struck and the heavier the weight that urged him down at each return. He lost his hold and fell the last few inches and immediately a wave had him, thrust him brutally into the angle then tried to tear him away. Between waves when he staggered to his feet the water was knee-deep over the pebbles and they gave beneath him. He fell on all fours and was hidden in a green heap that hit the back of the angle and climbed up in a tree-trunk of spray. He staggered round the angle then gripped with both hands. The water tore at him but he held on. He got his knife free and opened the blade. He ducked down and immediately there were visions of rock and weed in front of his eyes. The uproar of the sea sank to a singing note in the ears. Then he was up again, the knife swinging free, two limpets in his hands and the sea knocked him down and stood him on his head. He found rock and clung against the backwash. When the waves left him for a moment he opened his mouth and gasped in the air as though he were winning territory. He found holds in the angle and the sea exploded, thrust him up so that now his effort was to stay down and under control. After each blow he flattened himself to escape the descent of the water. As he rose the seas lost their quality of leaden power but became more personal and vicious. They tore at his clothing, they beat him in the crutch, they tented up his oilskin till the skirt was crumpled above his waist. If he looked down the

33

water came straight at his face, or hit him in the guts and thrust him up.

He came to the narrowest part and was shoved through. He opened his eyes after the water gushed back and breathed wetly as the foam streamed down his face. A lock of hair was plastered just to the bridge of his nose and he saw the end of it, double. The chute struck him again, the waterfall rushed back and he was still there, wedged by his weight in the narrowest part of the crevice where the funnel began and his body was shaking. He lay forward on the slope and began to straighten his legs. His face moved up against the rock and a torrent swept back over him. He began to fumble in the crumples of his oilskin. He brought out a limpet and set it on the rock by his waist. Water came again and went. He reversed his knife and tapped the limpet on the top with the haft. The limpet gave a tiny sideways lurch and sucked itself down against the rock. A weight pressed on him and the man and the limpet firmed down against the rock together.

His legs were straight and stiff and his eyes were shut. He brought his right arm round in a circle and felt above him. He found the blunted dent that was too smooth for a handhold. His hand came back, was inundated, fumbled in oilskin. He pulled it out and when the hand crawled round and up there was a limpet in the palm. The man was looking at the rock an inch or two from his face but without interest. What life was left was concentrated in the crawling right hand. The hand found the blunted hollow, and pitched the limpet beyond the edge. The body was lifted a few inches and lay motionless waiting for the return of the water. When the chute had passed the hand came back, took the knife, moved up and tapped blindly on rock. The fingers searched stiffly, found the limpet, hit with the haft of the knife.

He turned his face, endured another wave and considered the limpet above him gravely. His hand let the knife go, which slid and clattered and hung motionless by his waist. He took the tit of the lifebelt and unscrewed the end. The air breathed out and his body flattened a little in the funnel. He laid the side of his head down and did nothing. Before his mouth the wet surface of the rock was blurred a little and regularly the blur was erased by the return of the waterfall. Sometimes the pendant knife would clatter.

Again he turned his face and looked up. His fingers closed over the limpet. Now his right leg was moving. The toes searched tremulously for the first limpet as the fingers had searched for the second. They did not find the limpet but the knee did. The hand let go, came down to the knee and lifted that part of the leg. The snarl behind the stiff face felt the limpet as a pain in the crook of the knee. The teeth set. The whole body began to wriggle; the hand went back to the higher limpet and pulled. The man moved sideways up the slope of the roof. The left leg came in and the seaboot stocking pushed the first leg away. The side of the foot was against the limpet. The leg straightened. Another torrent returned and washed down.

The man was lying with one foot on a limpet, held mostly by friction. But his foot was on one limpet and the second one was before his eyes. He reached up and there was a possible handhold that his fingers found, provided the other one still gripped the limpet by his face. He moved up, up, up and then there was an edge for his fingers. His right arm rose, seized. He pulled with both arms, thrust with both legs. He saw a trench of rock beyond the edge, glimpsed sea, saw whiteness on the rocks and jumble. He fell forward.

He was lying in a trench. He could see a weathered wall
of rock and a long pool of water stretching away from his
eye. His body was in some other place that had nothing
to do with this landscape. It was splayed, scattered behind
him, his legs in different worlds, neck twisted. His right
arm was bent under his body and his wrist doubled. He
sensed this hand and the hard pressure of the knuckles
against his side but the pain was not intense enough to
warrant the titanic effort of moving. His left arm
stretched away along the trench and was half-covered in
water. His right eye was so close to this water that he
could feel a little pluck from the surface tension when he
blinked and his eyelashes caught in the film. The water
had flattened again by the time he saw the surface consciously but his right cheek and the corner of his mouth
were under water and were causing a tremble. The other
eye was above water and was looking down the trench.
The inside of the trench was dirty white, strangely white
with more than the glossy reflection from the sky. The
corner of his mouth pricked. Sometimes the surface of the

3

He was lying in a trench. He could see a weathered wall
of rock and a long pool of water stretching away from his
eye. His body was in some other place that had nothing
to do with this landscape. It was splayed, scattered behind
him, his legs in different worlds, neck twisted. His right
arm was bent under his body and his wrist doubled. He
sensed this hand and the hard pressure of the knuckles
against his side but the pain was not intense enough to
warrant the titanic effort of moving. His left arm
stretched away along the trench and was half-covered in
water. His right eye was so close to this water that he
could feel a little pluck from the surface tension when he
blinked and his eyelashes caught in the film. The water
had flattened again by the time he saw the surface consciously but his right cheek and the corner of his mouth
were under water and were causing a tremble. The other
eye was above water and was looking down the trench.
The inside of the trench was dirty white, strangely white
with more than the glossy reflection from the sky. The
corner of his mouth pricked. Sometimes the surface of the

water was pitted for a moment or two and faint, inter-lacing circles spread over it from each pit. His left eye watched them, looking through a kind of arch of darkness where the skull swept round the socket. At the bottom and almost a straight line, was the skin colour of his nose. Filling the arch was the level of shining water.

He began to think slowly.

I have tumbled in a trench. My head is jammed against the farther side and my neck is twisted. My legs must be up in the air over the other wall. My thighs are hurting because the weight of my legs is pushing against the edge of the wall as a fulcrum. My right toes are hurt more than the rest of my leg. My hand is doubled under me and that is why I feel the localized pain in my ribs. My fingers might be made of wood. That whiter white under the water along there is my hand, hidden.

There was a descending scream in the air, a squawk and the beating of wings. A gull was braking widely over the wall at the end of the trench, legs and claws held out. It yelled angrily at the trench, the wide wings gained a purchase and it hung flapping only a foot or two above the rock. Wind chilled his cheek. The webbed feet came up, the wings steadied and the gull side-slipped away. The commotion of its passage made waves in the white water that beat against his cheek, the shut eye, the corner of his mouth. The stinging increased.

There was no pain sharp enough to compel action. Even the stinging was outside the head. His left eye watched the whiter white of his hand under water. Some of the memory pictures came back. They were new ones of a man climbing up rock and placing limpets.

The pictures stirred him more than the stinging. They made his left hand contract under the surface and the oilskin arm roll in the water. His breathing grew suddenly fierce so that waves rippled away along the trench, crossed and came back. A ripple splashed into his mouth.

Immediately he was convulsed and struggling. His legs kicked and swung sideways. His head ground against rock and turned. He scrabbled in the white water with both hands and heaved himself up. He felt the too-smooth wetness running on his face and the brilliant jab of pain at the corner of his right eye. He spat and snarled. He glimpsed the trenches with their thick layers of dirty white, their trapped inches of solution, a gull slipping away over a green sea. Then he was forcing himself forward. He fell into the next trench, hauled himself over the wall, saw a jumble of broken rock, slid and stumbled. He was going down hill and he fell part of the way. There was moving water round flattish rocks, a complication of weedy life. The wind went down with him and urged him forward. As long as he went forward the wind was satisfied but if he stopped for a moment's caution it thrust his unbalanced body down so that he scraped and hit. He saw little of the open sea and sky or the whole rock but only flashes of intimate being, a crack or point, a hand's breadth of

yellowish surface that was about to strike a blow, unavoid-
able fists of rock that beat him impersonally, struck bright
flashes of light from his body. The pain in the corner of
his eye went with him too. This was the most important of
all the pains because it thrust a needle now into the dark
skull where he lived. The pain could not be avoided. His
body revolved round it. Then he was holding brown weed
and the sea was washing over his head and shoulders.
He pulled himself up and lay on a flat rock with a pool
across the top. He rolled the side of his face and his eye
backwards and forwards under water. He moved his hands
gently so that the water swished. They left the water and
reached round and gathered smears of green weed.

He knelt up and held the smears of green against his
eye and the right side of his face. He slumped back against
rock among the jellies and scalloped pitches and encamp-
ments of limpets and let the encrusted barnacles hurt him
as they would. He set his left hand gently on his thigh and
squinted sideways at it. The fingers were half-bent. The
skin was white with blue showing through and wrinkles
cut the surface in regular shapes. The needle reached after
him in the skull behind the dark arch. If he moved the eye-
ball the needle moved too. He opened his eye and it filled
immediately with water under the green weed.

He began to snort and make sounds deep in his chest.
They were like hard lumps of sound and they jerked him
as they came out. More salt water came out of each eye
and joined the traces of the sea and the solution on his

cheeks. His whole body began to shiver.

There was a deeper pool on a ledge farther down. He climbed slowly and heavily down, edged himself across and put his right cheek under again. He opened and closed his eye so that the water flushed the needle corner. The memory pictures had gone so far away that they could be disregarded. He felt round and buried his hands in the pool. Now and then a hard sound jerked his body.

The sea-gull came back with others and he heard them sounding their interlacing cries like a trace of their flight over his head. There were noises from the sea too, wet gurgles below his ear and the running thump of swells, blanketed by the main of the rock but still able to sidle round and send offshoots sideways among the rocks and into the crannies. The idea that he must ignore pain came and sat in the centre of his darkness where he could not avoid it. He opened his eyes for all the movement of the needle and looked down at his bleached hands. He began to mutter.

"Shelter. Must have shelter. Die if I don't."

He turned his head carefully and looked up the way he had come. The odd patches of rock that had hit him on the way down were visible now as part of each other. His eyes took in yards at a time, surfaces that swam as the needle pricked water out of him. He set himself to crawl back up the rock. The wind was lighter but dropping trails of rain still fell over him. He hauled himself up a cliff that was no higher than a man could span with his arms but it was an obstacle that had to be negotiated with much arrangement and thought for separate limbs. He lay for a while on the top of the little cliff and looked in watery snatches up the height of the rock. The sun lay just above the high part where the white trenches had waited for him. The light was struggling with clouds and rain-mist and there were birds wheeling across the rock. The sun was dull but drew more water from his eyes so that he screwed them up and cried out suddenly against the needle. He crawled by touch, and then with one eye through trenches and gullies where there was no whiteness. He lifted his legs over the broken walls of trenches as though they belonged to another body. All at once, with the diminishing of the pain in his eye, the cold and exhaustion came back. He fell flat in a gully and let his body look after itself. The deep chill fitted close to him, so close it was inside the clothes, inside the skin.

The chill and the exhaustion spoke to him clearly. Give up, they said, lie still. Give up the thought of return, the thought of living. Break up, leave go. Those white bodies are without attraction or excitement, the faces, the words, happened to another man in another place. An hour on this rock is a lifetime. What have you to lose? There is nothing here but torture. Give up. Leave go.

His body began to crawl again. It was not that there was muscular or nervous strength there that refused to be beaten but rather that the voices of pain were like waves beating against the sides of a ship. There was at

42

the centre of all the pictures and pains and voices a fact like a bar of steel, a thing—that which was so nakedly the centre of everything that it could not even examine itself. In the darkness of the skull, it existed, a darker dark, self-existent and indestructible.

"Shelter. Must have shelter."

The centre began to work. It endured the needle to look sideways, put thoughts together. It concluded that it must crawl this way rather than that. It noted a dozen places and rejected them, searched ahead of the crawling body. It lifted the luminous window under the arch, shifted the arch of skull from side to side like the slow shift of the head of a caterpillar trying to reach a new leaf. When the body drew near to a possible shelter the head still moved from side to side, moving more quickly than the slow thoughts inside.

There was a slab of rock that had slipped and fallen sideways from the wall of a trench. This made a triangular hole between the rock and the side and bottom of the trench. There was no more than a smear of rainwater in this trench and no white stuff. The hole ran away and down at an angle following the line of the trench and inside there was darkness. The hole even looked drier than the rest of the rock. At last his head stopped moving and he lay down before this hole as the sun dipped from view. He began to turn his body in the trench, among a complication of sodden clothing. He said nothing but breathed heavily with open mouth. Slowly he turned until his white

43

seaboot stockings were towards the crevice. He backed to the triangular opening and put his feet in. He lay flat on his stomach and began to wriggle weakly like a snake that cannot cast its skin. His eyes were open and unfocused. He reached back and forced the oilskin and duffle down on either side. The oilskin was hard and he backed with innumerable separate movements like a lobster backing into a deep crevice under water. He was in the crack up to his shoulders and rock held him tightly. He hutched the lifebelt up till the soft rubber was across the upper part of his chest. The slow thoughts waxed and waned, the eyes were empty except for the water that ran from the needle in the right one. His hand found the tit and he blew again slowly until the rubber was firmed up against his chest. He folded his arms, a white hand on either side. He let the left side of his face fall on an oilskinned sleeve and his eyes were shut—not screwed up but lightly closed. His mouth was still open, the jaw fallen sideways. Now and then a shudder came up out of the crack and set his head and arms shaking. Water ran slowly out of his sleeves, fell from his hair and his nose, dripped from the rucked-up clothing round his neck. His eyes fell open like the mouth because the needle was more controllable that way. Only when he had to blink them against water did the point jab into the place where he lived.

He could see gulls swinging over the rock, circling down. They settled and cried with erect heads and tongues, beaks wide open on the high point of the rock.

The sky greyed down and sea-smoke drifted over. The birds talked and shook their wings, folded them one over the other, settled like white pebbles against the rock and tucked in their heads. The greyness thickened into a darkness in which the few birds and the splashes of their dung were visible as the patches of foam were visible on the water. The trenches were full of darkness for down by the shelter for some reason there was no dirty white. The rocks were dim shapes among them. The wind blew softly and chill over the main rock and its unseen, gentle passage made a continual and almost inaudible hiss. Every now and then a swell thumped into the angle by the safety rock. After that there would be a long pause and then the rush and scramble of falling water down the funnel.

The man lay, huddled in his crevice, left cheek pillowed on black oilskin and his hands were glimmering patches on either side. Every now and then there came a faint scratching sound of oilskin as the body shivered.

4

The man was inside two crevices. There was first the rock, closed and not warm but at least not cold with the coldness of sea or air. The rock was negative. It confined his body so that here and there the shudders were beaten; not soothed but forced inward. He felt pain throughout most of his body but distant pain that was sometimes to be mistaken for fire. There was dull fire in his feet and a sharper sort in either knee. He could see this fire in his mind's eye because his body was a second and interior crevice which he inhabited. Under each knee, then, there was a little fire built with crossed sticks and busily flaring like the fire that is lighted under a dying camel. But the man was intelligent. He endured these fires although they gave not heat but pain. They had to be endured because to stand up or even move would mean nothing but an increase of pain—more sticks and more flame, extending under all the body. He himself was at the far end of this inner crevice of flesh. At this far end, away from the fires, there was a mass of him lying on a lifebelt that rolled backwards and forwards at every breath. Beyond the mass was the round, bone globe of the world and himself hanging inside. One half of this world burned and froze but with a steadier and bearable pain. Only towards the top half of this world there would sometimes come a jab that was like a vast needle prying after him. Then he would make seismic convulsions of whole continents on that side and the jabs would become frequent but less deep and the nature of that part of the globe would change. There would appear shapes of dark and grey in space and a patch of galactic whiteness that he knew vaguely was a hand connected to him. The other side of the globe was all dark and gave no offence. He floated in the middle of this globe like a waterlogged body. He knew as an axiom of existence that he must be content with the smallest of all small mercies as he floated there. All the extensions with which he was connected, their distant fires, their slow burning, their racks and pincers were at least far enough away. If he could hit some particular mode of inactive being, some subtlety of interior balance, he might be allowed by the nature of the second crevice to float, still and painless in the centre of the globe.

Sometimes he came near this. He became small, and the globe larger until the burning extensions were interplanetary. But this universe was subject to convulsions that began in deep space and came like a wave. Then he was larger again, filling every corner of the tunnels, sweeping with shrieking nerves over the fires, expanding in the globe until he filled it and the needle jabbed through the corner of his right eye straight into the darkness of his head. Dimly he would see one white hand while the pain stabbed. Then slowly he would sink back into the centre of the globe, shrink and float in the middle of a dark world. This became a rhythm that had obtained from all ages and would endure so.

This rhythm was qualified but not altered in essentials by pictures that happened to him and sometimes to someone else. They were brightly lit in comparison with the fires. There were waves larger than the universe and a glass sailor hanging in them. There was an order in neon lighting. There was a woman, not like the white detailed bodies but with a face. There was the gloom and hardness of a night-time ship, the lift of the deck, the slow cant and bumble. He was walking forward across the bridge to the binnacle and its dim light. He could hear Nat leaving his post as port look-out, Nat going down the ladder. He could hear that Nat had walking shoes on, not seaboots or plimsols. Nat was lowering his un-handy spider-length down the ladder with womanish care, not able now after all these months to wear the right clothes or negotiate a ladder like a seaman. Dawn had found him shivering from inadequate rig, the mess-deck would find him hurt by the language, a butt, humble, obedient and useless.

He looked briefly at the starboard horizon then across to the convoy, bulks just coming into view in the dawn light. They interrupted the horizon like so many bleak iron walls where now the long, blurred tears of rust were nearly visible.

But Nat would be fumbling aft, to find five minutes' solitude by the rail and meet his aeons. He would be picking his diffident way toward the depth-charge thrower on the starboard side not because it was preferable to the port rail but because he always went there. He would be enduring the wind and engine stink, the peculiar dusty dirt and shabbiness of a wartime destroyer because life itself with all its touches, tastes, sights and sounds and smells had been at a distance from him. He would go on enduring until custom made him indifferent. He would never find his feet in the Navy because those great feet of his had always been away out there, attached by accident while the man inside prayed and waited to meet his aeons.

But the deck-watch was ticking on to the next leg of the zigzag. He looked carefully at the second hand.

"Starboard fifteen."

Out on the port bow *Wildebeeste* was turning too. The grey light showed the swirl under her stern where the rudder had kicked across. As the bridge canted under him *Wildebeeste* seemed to slide astern from her position until she was lying parallel and just forrard of the beam.

"Midships."

Wildebeeste was still turning. Connected by the soles of his feet through steel to the long waver and roll of glaucous water he could predict to himself the exact degree of her list to port as she came round. But the water was not so predictable after all. In the last few degrees of her turn he saw a mound of grey, a seventh wave slide by her bows and pass under her. The swing of her stern increased, her stern slid down the slope and for that time she had carried ten degrees beyond her course, in a sudden lurch.

"Steady."

And curse the bloody Navy and the bloody war. He yawned sleepily and saw the swirl under *Wildebeeste*'s stern as she came back on course. The fires out there at the end of the second crevice flared up, a needle stabbed and he was back in his body. The fire died down again in the usual rhythm.

The destroyers in a V screen turned back together. Between orders he listened to the shivering ping of the Asdic and the light increased. The herd of merchantmen chugged on at six knots with the destroyers like outriders scouring the way before them, sweeping the sea clear with their invisible brooms, changing course together, all on one string.

He heard a step behind him on the ladder and busied himself to take a bearing because the captain might be coming. He checked the bearing of *Wildebeeste* with elaborate care. But no voice came with the steps.

He turned casually at last and there was Petty Officer Roberts—and now saluting.

"Good morning, Chief."

"Good morning, sir."

"What is it? Wangled a tot for me?"

The close eyes under their peak withdrew a little but the mouth made itself smile.

50

"Might, sir——"

And then, the calculation made, the advantage to self admitted, the smile widened.

"I'm a bit off me rum these days, somehow. Any time you'd care to——"

"O.K. Thanks."

And what now? A draft chit? Recommend for commission? Something small and manageable?

But Petty Officer Roberts was playing a game too deep. Whatever it was and wherever the elaborate system of obligations might lead to, it required nothing today but a grateful opinion of his good sense and understanding.

"About Walterson, sir."

Astonished laugh.

"My old friend Nat? What's he been doing? Not got himself in the rattle, has he?"

"Oh no, sir, nothing like that. Only——"

"What?"

"Well, just look now, sir, aft on the starboard side."

Together they walked to the starboard wing of the bridge. Nathaniel was still engaged with his aeons, feet held by friction on the corticene, bony rump on the rail just aft of the thrower. His hands were up to his face, his improbable length swaying with the scend of the swells.

"Silly ass."

"He'll do that once too often, sir."

Petty Officer Roberts came close. Liar. There was rum in his breath.

"I could have put him in the rattle for it, sir, but I thought, seeing he's a friend of yours in civvy street——"

Pause.

"O.K., Chief. I'll drop him a word myself."

"Thank you, sir."

"Thank *you*, Chief."

"I won't forget the tot, sir."

"Thanks a lot."

Petty Officer Roberts saluted and withdrew from the presence. He descended the ladder.

"Port fifteen."

Solitude with fires under the knees and a jabbing needle. Solitude out over the deck where the muzzle of X gun was lifted over the corticene. He smiled grimly to himself and reconstructed the inside of Nathaniel's head. He must have laid aft, hopefully, seeking privacy between the crew of the gun and the depth-charge watch. But there was no solitude for a rating in a small ship unless he was knowing enough to find himself a quiet number. He must have drifted aft from the mob of the fo'castle, from utter, crowded squalor to a modified and windy form of it. He was too witless to understand that the huddled mess-deck was so dense as to ensure a form of privacy, like that a man can achieve in a London crowd. So he would endure the gloomy stare of the depth-charge watch at his prayers, not understanding that they would keep an eye on him because they had nothing else to do.

"Midships. Steady."

Zig.

And he is praying in his time below when he ought to be turned in, swinging in his hammock, because he has been told that on watch he must keep a look-out over a sector of the sea. So he kept a look-out, dutiful and uncomprehending.

The dark centre of the head turned, saw the port look-out hutched, the swinging RDF aerial, the funnel with its tremble of hot air and trace of fume, looked down over the break of the bridge to the starboard deck.

Nathaniel was still there. His improbable height, combined with the leanness that made it seem even more incredible, had reduced the rail to an insecure parapet. His legs were splayed out and his feet held him by friction against the deck. As the dark centre watched, it saw Nathaniel take his hands down from his face, lay hold of the rail and get himself upright. He began to work his way forrard over the deck, legs straddled, arms out for balance. He carried his absurd little naval cap exactly level on the top of his head, and his curly black hair—a trifle lank for the night's dampness—emerged from under it all round. He saw the bridge by chance and gravely brought his right hand toward the right side of his head—taking no liberties, thought the black centre, knowing his place, humble aboard as in civvy street, ludicrous, unstoppable.

But the balance of the thin figure was disturbed by this temporary exercise of the right hand; it tottered sideways, tried for the salute again, missed, considered the problem gravely with arms out and legs astraddle. A scend made it rock. It turned, went to the engine casing, tried out the surface to see if the metal was hot, steadied, turned forrard and slowly saluted the bridge.

The dark centre made itself wave cheerfully to the foreshortened figure. Nathaniel's face altered even at that distance. The delight of recognition appeared in it, not plastered on and adjusted as Petty Officer Roberts had smiled under his too-close eyes: but rising spontaneously from the conjectural centre behind the face, evidence of sheer niceness that made the breath come short with maddened liking and rage. There was a convulsion in the substrata of the globe at this end so that the needle came stabbing and prying towards the centre that had floated all this while without pain.

He seized the binnacle and the rock and cried out in an anguish of frustration.

"Can't anyone understand how I feel?"

Then he was extended again throughout the tunnels of the inner crevice and the fires were flaring and spitting in his flesh.

There came a new noise among the others. It was connected with the motionless blobs of white out there. They were more definite than they had been. Then he was aware that time had passed. What had seemed an eternal rhythm had been hours of darkness and now there was a faint light that consolidated his personality, gave it bounds

54

and sanity. The noise was a throaty cluck from one of the roosting gulls.

He lay with the pains, considering the light and the fact of a new day. He could inspect his wooden left hand if he was careful about the management of the inflamed corner of his eye. He willed the fingers to close and they quivered, then contracted. Immediately he was back in them, he became a man who was thrust deep into a crevice in barren rock. Knowledge and memory flowed back in orderly succession, he remembered the funnel, the trench. He became a castaway in broad daylight and the necessity of his position fell on him. He began to heave at his body, dragging himself out of the space between the rocks. As he moved out, the gulls clamoured out of sleep and took off. They came back, sweeping in to examine him with sharp cries then sidling away in the air again. They were not like the man-wary gulls of inhabited beaches and cliffs. Nor had they about them the primal innocence of unvisited nature. They were wartime gulls who, finding a single man with water round him, resented the warmth of his flesh and his slow, unwarranted movements. They told him, with their close approach, and flapping hover that he was far better dead, floating in the sea like a burst hammock. He staggered and struck out among them with wooden arms.

"Yah! Get away! Bugger off!"

They rose clamorously wheeling, came back till their wings beat his face. He struck out again in panic so that one went drooping off with a wing that made no more than a half-beat. They retired then, circled and watched. Their heads were narrow. They were flying reptiles. An ancient antipathy for things with claws set him shuddering at them and thinking into their smooth outlines all the strangeness of bats and vampires.

"Keep off! Who do you think I am?"

Their circles widened. They flew away to the open sea.

He turned his attention back to his body. His flesh seemed to be a compound of aches and stiffnesses. Even the control system had broken down for his legs had to be given deliberate and separate orders as though they were some unhandy kind of stilts that had been strapped to him. He broke the stilts in the middle, and got upright. He discovered new fires—little islands of severer pain in the general ache. The one at the corner of his right eye was so near to him that he did not need to discover it. He stood up, leaning his back against the side of a trench and looked round him.

The morning was dull but the wind had died down and the water was leaping rather than progressing. He became aware of a new thing; sound of the sea that the sailor never hears in his live ship. There was a gentle undertone compounded of countless sloppings of wavelets, there was a constant gurgling and sucking that ranged from a stony smack to a ruminative swallow. There were sounds that seemed every moment to be on the point of articulation but lapsed into a liquid slapping like appetite. Over all this was a definable note, a singing hiss, soft touch of the air

56

on stone, continuous, subtle, unending friction.

A gull-cry swirled over him and he raised an arm and looked under the elbow but the gull swung away from the rock. When the cry had gone everything was gentle again, non-committal and without offence.

He looked down at the horizon and passed his tongue over his upper lip. It came again, touched experimentally, vanished. He swallowed. His eyes opened wider and he paid no attention to the jab. He began to breathe quickly.

"Water!"

As in the sea at a moment of desperate crisis his body changed, became able and willing. He scrambled out of the trench on legs that were no longer wooden. He climbed across fallen buttresses that had never supported anything but their own weight; he slithered in the white pools of the trenches near the top of the rock. He came to the edge of the cliff where he had climbed and a solitary gull slipped away from under his feet. He worked himself round on his two feet but the horizon was like itself at every point. He could only tell when he had inspected every point by the lie of the rock beneath him. He went round again.

At last he turned back to the rock itself and climbed down but more slowly now from trench to trench. When he was below the level of the white bird-droppings he stopped and began to examine the rock foot by foot. He crouched in a trench, gripping the lower side and looking at every part of it with quick glances as if he were trying to follow the flight of a hover-fly. He saw water on a flat rock, went to it, put his hands on either side of the puddle and stuck his tongue in. His lips contracted down round his tongue, sucked. The puddle became nothing but a patch of wetness on the rock. He crawled on. He came to a horizontal crack in the side of a trench. Beneath the crack a slab of rock was falling away and there was water caught. He put his forehead against the rock then turned sideways until his cheek rested above the crack—but still his tongue could not reach the water. He thrust and thrust, mouth ground against the stone but still the water was beyond him. He seized the cracked stone and jerked furiously until it broke away. The water spilled down and became a film in the bottom of the trench. He stood there, heart thumping and held the broken stone in his hands.

"Use you loaf, man. Use your loaf."

He looked down the jumbled slope before him. He began to work the rock methodically. He noticed the broken stone in his hands and dropped it. He worked across the rock and back from trench to trench. He came on the mouldering bones of fish and a dead gull, its up-turned breast-bone like the keel of a derelict boat. He found patches of grey and yellow lichen, traces even of earth, a button of moss. There were the empty shells of crabs, pieces of dead weed, and the claws of a lobster.

At the lower end of the rock there were pools of water but they were salt. He came back up the slope, his needle and the fires forgotten. He groped in the crevice where he had lain all night but the rock was nearly dry. He clambered over the fallen slab of stone that had sheltered him.

The slab was in two pieces. Once there must have been a huge upended layer of rock that had endured while the others weathered away. It had fallen and broken in two. The larger piece lay across the trench at the very edge of the rock. Part of it projected over the sea, and the trench led underneath like a gutter.

He lay down and inserted himself. He paused. Then he was jerking his tail like a seal and lifting himself forward with his flippers. He put his head down and made sucking noises. Then he lay still.

The place in which he had found water was like a little cave. The floor of the trench sloped down gently under water so that this end of the pool was shallow. There was room for him to lie with his elbows spread apart for the slab had smashed down the wall on the right-hand side. The roof stone lay across at an angle and the farther end of the cave was not entirely stopped up. There was a small hole high up by the roof, full of daylight and a patch of sky. The light from the sky was reflected in and from the water so that faint lines quivered over the stone roof. The water was drinkable but there was no pleasure in the taste. It tasted of things that were vaguely unpleasant though the tastes were not individually identifiable. The water did not satisfy thirst so much as allay it. There seemed to be plenty of the stuff, for the pool was yards long before him and the farther end looked deep. He lowered his head and sucked again. Now that his one and a half eyes were adjusted to the light he could see there was a deposit under the water, reddish and slimy. The deposit was not hard but easily disturbed so that where he had drunk, the slime was coiling up, drifting about, hanging, settling. He watched dully.

Presently he began to mutter.

"Rescue. See about rescue."

He struggled back with a thump of his skull against rock. He crawled along the trench and clambered to the top of the rock and peered round and round the horizon again. He knelt and lowered himself on his hands. The thoughts began to flicker quickly in his head.

"I cannot stay up here all the time. I cannot shout to them if they pass. I must make a man to stand here for me. If they see anything like a man they will come closer."

There was a broken rock below his hands, leaning against the wall from which the clean fracture had fallen. He climbed down and wrestled with a great weight. He made the stone rise on an angle; he quivered and the stone fell over. He collapsed and lay for a while. He left the stone and scrambled heavily down to the little cliff and the scattered rocks where he had bathed his eye. He found an encrusted boulder lying in a rock pool and pulled it up. He got the stone against his stomach, staggered for a few steps, dropped the stone, lifted and carried again. He dumped the stone on the high point above the funnel and came back. There was a stone like a suitcase balanced on

60

the wall of a trench and he pondered what he should do. He put his back against the suitcase and his feet against the other side of the trench. The suitcase grated, moved. He got a shoulder under one end and heaved. The suitcase tumbled in the next trench and broke. He grinned without humour and lugged the larger part up into his lap. He raised the broken suitcase to the wall, turned it end over end, engineered it up slopes of fallen but unmanageable rock, pulled and hauled.

Then there were two rocks on the high part, one with a trace of blood. He looked once round the horizon and climbed down the slope again. He stopped, put a hand to his forehead, then examined the palm. But there was no blood.

He spoke out loud in a voice that was at once flat and throaty.

"I am beginning to sweat."

He found a third stone but could not get it up the wall of the trench. He retreated with it, urged it along the bottom to a lower level until he could find an exit low enough for him to heave it up. By the time he had dragged it to the others his hands were broken. He knelt by the stones and considered the sea and sky. The sun was out wanly and there were fewer layers of cloud. He lay down across the three stones and let them hurt him. The sun shone on his left ear from the afternoon side of the rock.

He got up, put the second stone laboriously on the third and the first on the second. The three stones measured nearly two feet from top to bottom. He sat down and leaned back against them. The horizon was empty, the sea gentle, the sun a token. A sea-gull was drifting over the water a stone's throw from the rock, and now the bird was rounded, white and harmless. He covered his aching eye with one hand to rest it but the effort of holding a hand up was too much and he let the palm fall back on his knee. He ignored his eye and tried to think.

"Food?"

He got to his feet and climbed down over the trenches. At the lower end were cliffs a few feet high and beyond them separate rocks broke the surface. He ignored these for the moment because they were inaccessible. The cliffs were very rough. They were covered with a crust of tiny barnacles that had welded their limy secretions into an extended colony that dipped down in the water as deep as his better eye could see. There were yellowish limpets and coloured sea-snails drying and drawn in against the rock. Each limpet sat in the hollow its foot had worn. There were clusters of blue mussels too, with green webs of weed caught over them. He looked back up the side of the rock—under the water-hole for he could see the roof slab projecting like a diving-board—and saw how the mussels had triumphed over the whole wall. Beneath a defined line the rock was blue with them. He lowered himself carefully and inspected the cliff. Under water the harvest of food was even thicker for the mussels were bigger down there and water-snails were crawling over them. And among the limpets, the mussels, the snails and barnacles, dotted like sucked sweets, were the red blobs of jelly, the anemones. Under water they opened their mouths in a circle of petals but up by his face, waiting for the increase of the tide they were pursed up and slumped like breasts when the milk has been drawn from them.

Hunger contracted under his clothes like a pair of hands. But as he hung there, his mouth watering, a lump rose in his throat as if he were very sad. He hung on the creamy wall and listened to the washing of water, the minute ticks and whispers that came from this abundant, but not quite vegetable, life. He felt at his waist, produced the lanyard, swung it and caught the knife with his free hand. He put the blade against his mouth, gripped with his teeth and pulled the haft away from it. He put the point under a limpet and it contracted down so that he felt its muscular strength as he turned the blade. He dropped the knife to the length of the lanyard and caught the limpet as it fell. He turned the limpet over in his hand and peered into the broad end. He saw an oval brown foot drawn in, drawn back, shutting out the light.

"Bloody hell."

He jerked the limpet away from him and the tent made a little flip of water in the sea. As the ripples died away he watched it waver down whitely out of sight. He looked for a while at the place where the limpet had disappeared. He took his knife again and began to chisel lines among the barnacles. They wept and bled salty, uretic water. He poked an anemone with the point of the knife and the jelly screwed up tight. He pressed the top with the flat of the blade and the opening pissed in his eye. He jammed the knife against the rock and shut it. He climbed back and sat on the high rock with his back against the three stones—two broken and an encrusted one on top.

Inside, the man was aware of a kind of fit that seized his body. He drew his feet up against him and rolled sideways so that his face was on the rock. His body was jumping and shuddering beneath the sodden clothing. He whispered against stone.

"You can't give up."

Immediately he began to crawl away down hill. The crawl became a scramble. Down by the water he found stones but they were of useless shape. He chose one from just under water and toiled back to the others. He changed the new one for the top stone, grated it into place, then put the encrusted one back. Two feet, six inches.

He muttered.

"Must. Must."

He climbed down to the rock-side opposite the cliff of mussels. There were ledges on this side and water sucking up and down. The water was very dark and there was long weed at the bottom, straps like the stuff travellers sometimes put round suitcases when the locks are broken. This brown weed was collapsed and coiled over itself near the surface but farther out it lay upright in the water or moved slowly like tentacles or tongues. Beyond that there was nothing but the blackness of deep water going down to the bottom of the deep sea. He took his eyes away from this, climbed along one of the ledges, but everywhere the rock was firm and there were no separated pieces to be found, though in one place the solid ledge was cracked. He pushed at this part with his stockinged feet but could not move it. He turned clumsily on the ledge and came back. At the lower end of the great rock he found the stones with the wrong shape and took them one by one to a trench and piled them. He pried in crevices and pulled out blocks and rounded masses of yellowing quartz on which the weed was draggled like green hair. He took them to the man he was building and piled them round the bottom stone. Some were not much bigger than potatoes and he knocked these in where the big stones did not fit until the top one no longer rocked when he touched it. He put one last stone on the others, one big as his head.

Three feet.

He stood away from the pile and looked round him. The pile reached in his view from horizon level to higher than the sun. He was astonished when he saw this and looked carefully to establish where west was. He saw the outlying rock that had saved him and the sea-gulls were floating just beyond the backwash.

He climbed down the rock again to where he had prised off the limpet. He made a wry face and pushed his doubled fists into the damp cloth over his belly. He hung on the little cliff and began to tear away the blobs of red jelly with his fingers. He set them on the edge of the cliff and did not look at them for a while. Then he turned his one and a half eyes down to them and inspected them closely. They lay like a handful of sweets only they moved ever so slightly and there was a little clear water trickling from the pile. He sat by them on the edge of the cliff and no longer saw them. His face set in a look of agony.

"Bloody hell!"

His fingers closed over a sweet. He put it quickly in his mouth, ducked, swallowed, shuddered. He took another, swallowed, took another as fast as he could. He bolted the pile of sweets then sat rigid, his throat working. He subsided, grinning palely. He looked down at his left hand and there was one last sweet lying against his little finger in a drip of water. He clapped his hand to his mouth, stared over the fingers and fought with his stomach. He scrambled over the rocks to the water-hole and pulled himself in. Again the coils of red silt and slime rose from the bottom. There was a band of red round the nearer end of the pool that was about half an inch across.

When he had settled his stomach with the harsh water he came out of the hole backwards. The sea-gulls were circling the rock now and he looked at them with hate.

"You won't get me!"

He clambered back to the top of the rock where his three-foot dwarf stood. The horizon was in sight all round and empty. He licked a trace of drinkable water from his lips.

"I have enough to drink———"

He stood, looking down at the slab over his drinking water where it projected like a diving-board. He went slowly to the cliff, got down and peered under the slab. The seaward end of the pool was held back by a jumble of broken stones that were lodged against each other. Behind the impaired window of his sight he saw the red silt rising and coiling. The stuff must lie over the inner side of these stones, sealing them lightly against the water's escape. He had a quick vision of the hidden surfaces, holes that time had furred with red till they were stopped and the incongruous fresh water held back among all the salt; but held back so delicately that the merest touch would set his life irrevocably flowing———

He backed away with staring eyes and breath that came quick.

"Forget it!"

He began to thrust himself backwards into the sleeping crevice. He got almost to his ears out of sight and filled the hole with his body and heavy clothing. He pulled the sleeves of his duffle out of the oilskin tubes until they came over the backs of his hands. After a little struggling he could grip them with his fingers and double his fists so that they were hidden in the hairy duffle. The lifebelt supported his chest and throat once more and he pillowed his left cheek on his forearm. He lay so, shivering now that the sun had gone down, while the green sky turned blue, dark blue and the gulls floated down. His body yielded to the shivers but between the bouts it lay quite still. His mouth was open and his eyes stared anxiously into the darkness. Once, he jerked and the mouth spoke.

"Forget it!"

A gull moved a little then settled down again.

5

But he could not fall into the pit because he was extended through his body. He was aware dimly of returning strength; and this not only allowed him to savour the cold and be physically miserable but to be irritated by it. Instead of the apocalyptic visions and voices of the other night he had now nothing but ill-used and complaining flesh. The point of the needle in his eye was blunted but instead of enduring anything rather than its stab he had continually to rub one foot over the other or press with his body against the slab of rock in an effort to shut off the chill on that side, only to find that the other side required attention more and more insistently. He would heave the globe of darkness in which he most lived off a hard, wooden surface, rotate it and lay the other hemisphere down. There was another difference between this night and the last. The fires had died down but they were still there now he had the time and the strength to attend to them. The stiffness had become a settled sense of strain as if his body were being stretched mercilessly. The rock too, now that he had a little strength to spare was forcing additional discomfort on him. What the globe had taken in its extreme exhaustion for a smooth surface was in fact undulating with the suggestion of prominences here and there. These suggestions became localized discomforts that changed in turn to a dull ache. Allowed to continue, aches became pains then fires that must be avoided. So he would heave his thigh away or wriggle weakly only to find that the prominence was gone and had left nothing but an undulation. His thigh would flatten down again and wait in the darkness for the discomfort, the ache, the pain, the fire.

Up at the top end now that the window was dark the man found the intermissions of discomfort were again full of voices and things that could not but be seen. He had a confused picture of the passage of the sun below him beyond the central fires of the earth. But both the sun and the fires were too far away to warm him. He saw the red silt holding back the fresh water, a double handful of red sweets, an empty horizon.

"I shall live!"

He saw the sun below him with its snail movement and was confused inside his head by the earth's revolution on its axis and its year-long journey round the sun. He saw how many months a man must endure before he was warmed by the brighter light of spring. He watched the sun for months without thought or identity. He saw it from many angles, through windows of trains or from fields. He confused its fires with other fires, on allotments, in gardens, in grates. One of these fires was most insistent that here was reality and to be watched. The fire was behind the bars of a grate. He found that the grate was in a room and then everything became familiar out of the past and he knew where he was and that the time and the words were significant. There was a tall and spider-thin figure sitting in the chair opposite. It looked up under its black curls, as if it were consulting a reference book on the other side of the ceiling.

"Take us as we are now and heaven would be sheer negation. Without form and void. You see? A sort of black lightning destroying everything that we call life."

But he was laughing and happy in his reply.

"I don't see and I don't much care but I'll come to your lecture. My dear Nathaniel, you've no idea how glad I am to see you!"

Nathaniel looked his face over carefully.

"And I, too. About seeing you, I mean."

"We're showing emotion, Nat, We're being un-English."

Again the careful look.

"I think you need my lecture. You're not happy, are you?"

"I'm not really interested in heaven either. Let me get you a drink."

"No, thanks."

Nathaniel uncoiled from the chair and stood with his arms out on either side, hands bent up. He looked, first at nothing, then round the room. He went to the wall and perched himself absurdly high up with his bony rump on the top of a shelf. He pushed his incredible legs out and splayed them apart till he was held insecurely by the friction of the soles of his feet. He looked up at the reference book again.

"You could call it a talk on the technique of dying."

"You'll die a long time before me. It's a cold night—and look how you're dressed!"

Nathaniel peered at the laughing window then down at himself.

"Is it? Yes. I suppose I am."

"And I'm going to have a damned long life and get what I'm after."

"And that is——?"

"Various things."

"But you're not happy."

"Why do you spill this over me, of all people?"

"There's a connection between us. Something will happen to us or perhaps we were meant to work together. You have an extraordinary capacity to endure."

"To what end?"

"To achieve heaven."

"Negation?"

"The technique of dying into heaven."

"No thanks. Be your age, Nat."

"You could, you know. And I——"

Nat's face was undergoing a change. It turned towards him again. The flush on the cheeks was painful. The eyes loomed and impended.

"—And I, have a feeling. Don't laugh, please—but I feel—you could say that I know." Below the eyes the breath came out in a little gasp. Feet scraped.

"—You could say that I know it is important for you personally to understand about heaven—about dying— because in only a few years———"

For a while there was silence, a double shock—for the bells ceased to toll beyond the windows of the room as though they had stopped with the voice. A vicious sting from his cigarette whipped along the arm into the globe so that he flicked it away and cried out. Then he was flat on the floor, fumbling for the stub under the armchair and the undulations of the floor were a discomfort to the body. Lying there, the words pursued him, made his ears buzz, set up a tumult, pushed his heart to thump with sudden, appalled understanding as though it were gasping the words that Nathaniel had not spoken.

"—because in only a few years you will be dead."

He cried out against the unspoken words in fury and panic.

"You bloody fool, Nat! You awful bloody fool!"

The words echoed in the trench and he jerked his cheek up off the oilskin. There was much light outside, sunlight and the crying of gulls.

He shouted.

"I'm damned if I'll die!"

He hauled himself quickly out of the crevice and stood

73

in the trench. The sea and sky were dark blue and the sun was high enough not to make a dazzle from the water. He felt the sun on his face and rubbed with both hands at the bristles. He looked quickly round the horizon then climbed down to a trench. He began to fumble with his trousers, glancing furtively behind him. Then for the first time on the rock he broke up the bristly, external face with a shout of jeering laughter. He went back to the dwarf and made water in a hosing gesture at the horizon.

"Gentlemen are requested to adjust their dress before leaving."

He began to fumble with the buttons of his oilskin and lugged it off fiercely. He picked and pulled at the tapes that held his lifebelt inside the duffle. He slipped both off and dumped them in a heavy heap and stood there looking down. He glanced at the two wavy lines of gold braid on either arm, the gilt buttons, the black doeskin of his jacket and trousers. He peeled himself, jacket, woollen sweater, black sweater, shirt, vest; pulled off his long stockings, his socks, his pants. He stood still and examined what he could see of his body.

The feet had been so thoroughly sodden that they seemed to have lost their shape. One big toe was blue and black with bruise and drying blood. There were bruises on either knee that ended in lacerations, not cuts or jabs but places the size of a sixpence where the skin and flesh had been worn off. His right hip was blue as though someone had laid a hand dipped in paint on it.

He examined his arms. The right elbow was swollen and stiff and there were more bruises about. Here and there on his body were patches, not of raw flesh but of blood flecks under the skin. He felt the bristles on his face tenderly. His right eye was fogged and that cheek was hot and stiff.

He took his vest and tried to wring out the body but there was water held in the material that would not come free. He put his left foot on one end of the twisted cloth and screwed the other with both hands. Dampness appeared and moistened the rock. He did this in turn to each piece of clothing and spread the lot in the sun to dry. He sat down by the dwarf, fumbled in his jacket and brought out a sodden packet of papers and a small brown booklet. The colour had run from the booklet and stained the papers as if they were rusting. He spread the papers out round him and rummaged through his pockets in turn. He found two pennies and a florin. He laid them by the dwarf in a little heap. He took his knife on its lanyard from the pocket of his oilskin and hung it round his neck. When he had done that he put up his hand and tugged gently at the small brown disc that was tied round his neck by a white thread. He bent his face into a grin. He got up and scrambled over the rocks to the water-hole. He eased himself in and leaned forward. The red coils rose and reminded him of the other tamped end of the pool. He backed out carefully, holding his breath.

He climbed down over the trenches to the lower end of

the rock. The water was low and tons of living jelly was spread in armour over the cliffs. Where he stood with his toes projecting over the edge the food was dry, and talked with continual tiny crepitations. The weed was transparent over the shells and only faintly green. He clambered down from handhold to handhold, wincing as he caught the sharp shells with his feet. He pulled at mussels but they would not come away. He had to twist them out as if he were breaking bones away from their tendons, screwing them out of the joints. He jerked them over his head so that they arched up and fell clattering on the rock. He worked among the sharp shells over the wavering water until his legs were trembling with strain. He climbed the cliff, rested, came back and twisted out more. There was a scattered harvest of them on the rock, some of them four inches long. He sat down, breathless in the sun and worked at them. They were not vulnerable like the red sweets; they were gripped and glued tight and there was nowhere to get the blade of the knife in. He put one on the rock and beat it with the haft of his knife until the shell fractured. He took out the complicated body and looked away over the sea.

"The Belgians do."

He gulped the body down. He set his teeth, broke another shell. Soon he had a heap of raw flesh that lay, white and yellow on the dry rock. His jaws moved, he looked away at the horizon. The fogged side of his right eye was pulled slightly as he ate. He felt round with his hand and the heap was gone. He climbed down the cliff and got more. He opened each of these with a sudden downward jab of his knife. When they were gone he forced the red sweets from the rock and popped them in his mouth. He made no distinction between green and red. He took a wisp of green seaweed and chewed it like a leaf of lettuce. He went back to the water-hole, inserted himself and lay for a moment, looking down at the gleaming surface. He moistened his lips, so that the coils of red slime only stirred a little then lay down again. He eased himself out, clambered to the top of the rock and looked round. The horizon was ruled straight and hard in every part. He sat down.

The papers and booklet were still damp but he took up the booklet and opened it. Inside the cover was a transparent guard over a photograph. He peered through the cover and made out a fogged portrait. He could see a carefully arranged head of hair, a strong and smiling face, the white silk scarf round the neck. But detail had gone for ever. The young man who smiled dimly at him through fog and brown stains was distant as the posed portraits of great-grandparents in a faint, brown world.

Even so, he continued to look, searching for the details he remembered rather than saw, touching his bristled cheek while he divined the smiling smoothness of the one before him, rearranging the unkempt hair, feeling tenderly the painful corner of an eye. Opposite the photograph was writing in a slot but this too was smeared and washed into

77

illegibility. He put the booklet down and felt for the brown disc hanging round his neck. He lifted the disc as far as the string would allow until it was close to his left eye. He strained back and got it far enough away from him.

CHRISTOPHER

HADLEY

MARTIN

TY. LIEUT., R.N.V.R.

C. OF E.

He read the inscription again and again, cut by cut. His lips began to move. He dropped the disc, looked down at his salted legs with their scars, at his belly and the bush of hair over his privates.

He spoke out loud, using his voice hoarsely and with a kind of astonishment.

"Christopher Hadley Martin. Martin. Chris. I am what I always was!"

All at once it seemed to him that he came out of his curious isolation inside the globe of his head and was extended normally through his limbs. He lived again on the surface of his eyes, he was out in the air. Daylight crowded down on him, sunlight, there was a sparkle on the sea. The solid rock was coherent as an object, with layered guano, with fresh water and shell-fish. It was a position in a finite sea at the intersection of two lines, there were real ships passing under the horizon. He got quickly to his feet and laboured round the rock, turning his clothes in the sun.

He sniffed the pants and laughed. He went back to the papers and turned them. He took up the coins, chinked them in his hand for a moment and made as if to toss them in the sea. He paused.

"That would be too cracker-motto. Too ham."

He looked at the quiet sea.

"I don't claim to be a hero. But I've got health and education and intelligence. I'll beat you."

The sea said nothing. He grinned a little foolishly at himself.

"What I meant was to affirm my determination to survive. And of course, I'm talking to myself."

He looked round the rock.

"The first thing to do is to survey the estate."

The rock had diminished from an island to a thing. In the sunlight and absence of cold the whole could be inspected not only with eyes but with understanding. He saw at once that the trenches were the worn ends of vertical strata and the walls between them, harder layers that had worn more slowly. They were the broken end of a deep bed of mud that had been compressed by weight until the mud had heated and partly fused. Some convulsion of the upper layers, an unguessable contortion, a gripe of the earth's belly had torn the deep bed and thrust this broken end up vertically through mud and clay until it erupted as the tooth bursts out of the fleshy jaw. Then the less compressed layers had worn away into trenches full of edges like the cut pages of a book. The walls too were broken in

79

places and modified everywhere by local hazard. Some of the walls had fallen and lay jumbled in the trenches. The whole top of the rock tended down, trench by trench, from the west to the east.

The cliff sides of the rock concealed the stratification for they were water-worn and fretted into lace by the plant-animals that clustered so thickly on them. This top was concreted with whiteness under stinking water but down there where the blue and shattered mussel-shells lay scattered, the rock was clean or covered with barnacles and weed. Beyond the rock was a gap of shallow water, then another smaller rock, another and another in a slightly curving line. Then there was a pock that interrupted the pattern of the water and after that, the steep climb of the sea up to the sky.

He looked solemnly at the line of rocks and found himself thinking of them as teeth. He caught himself imagining that they were emerging gradually from the jaw—but that was not the truth. They were sinking; or rather they were being worn away in infinite slow motion. They were the grinders of old age, worn away. A lifetime of the world had blunted them, was reducing them as they ground what food rocks eat.

He shook his head irritably then caught his breath at the sudden pain in his neck.

"The process is so slow it has no relevance to——"

He stopped. He looked up into the air, then round over his shoulder. He repeated the words carefully, with the same intonation and at the same strength.

"The process is so slow——"

There was something peculiar about the sound that came out of his mouth. He discounted the hoarseness as of a man recovering from a cold or a bout of violent shouting. That was explicable.

He sang loudly.

"Alouette, gentille Alouette——"

He held his nose with his right hand and tried to blow through it until the pressure rounded his cheeks. Nothing cracked in his ears. His eyes hurt and water ran round them. He bent down, put his hands on his scarred knees and turned his head sideways. He shook his head violently, ignoring the pain in his neck and hoping to feel the little wobbling weight that would tell of water caught in his ears.

He stood up, facing a whole amphitheatre of water and sang a scale.

"Lah-la, la, la, la, la la-lah!"

The sound ended at his mouth.

He struck an attitude and declaimed.

> *The weary moon with her lamp before*
> *Knocks even now upon dawn's grey door——*

His voice faltered and stopped. He brought his hand down, turned the wrist, held the palm about a foot in front of his mouth.

"Testing. Testing. I am receiving you, strength——"

He closed his lips, lowered his hand slowly. The blue, igloo-roof over the rock went away to a vast distance, the visible world expanded with a leap. The water lopped round a tiny rock in the middle of the Atlantic. The strain tautened his face. He took a step among the scattered papers.

"My God!"

He gripped the stone dwarf, clutched himself to the humped shoulders and stared across. His mouth was open again. His heart-beats were visible as a flutter among the ribs. The knuckles of his hands whitened.

There was a clatter from the dwarf. The head stone thumped and went knock, knock, knock down the cliff.

Flumf.

He began to curse. He scrambled down the rock, found a too heavy stone, moved it about a yard and then let go. He threw himself over the stone and went cursing to the water. But there was nothing visible within reach that he could handle. He went quickly to the top again and stood looking at the headless dwarf in terror. He scrambled back to the too heavy stone and fought with it. He moved it, end over end. He built steps to the top of a wall and worked the great stone up. He drew from his body more strength than he had got. He bled. He stood sweating among the papers at last. He dismantled the dwarf and re-built him on the stone that after all was not too heavy for education and intelligence and will.

Four feet.

He jammed in the dry, white potatoes.

"Out of this nettle danger——"

The air sucked up his voice like blotting-paper.

Take a grip.

Education and intelligence.

He stood by the dwarf and began to talk like a man who has an unwilling audience but who will have his say whether anyone listens to him or not.

6

"The end to be desired is rescue. For that, the bare minimum necessary is survival. I must keep this body going. I must give it drink and food and shelter. When I do that it does not matter if the job is well done or not so long as it is done at all. So long as the thread of life is unbroken it will connect a future with the past for all this ghastly interlude. Point one.

"Point two. I must expect to fall sick. I cannot expose the body to this hardship and expect the poor beast to behave as if it were in clover. I must watch for signs of sickness and doctor myself.

"Point three. I must watch my mind. I must not let madness steal up on me and take me by surprise. Already—I must expect hallucinations. That is the real battle. That is why I shall talk out loud for all the blotting-paper. In normal life to talk out loud is a sign of insanity. Here it is proof of identity.

"Point four. I must help myself to be rescued. I cannot do anything but be visible. I have not even a stick to hoist a shirt on. But one will come within sight of this rock without turning a pair of binoculars on it. If they see the rock they will see this dwarf I have made. They will know that someone built the dwarf and they will come and take me off. All I have to do is to live and wait. I must keep my grip on reality."

He looked firmly at the sea. All at once he found that he was seeing through a window again. He was inside himself at the top end. The window was bounded above by the mixed, superimposed skin and hair of both brows, and divided into three lights by two outlines or shadows of noses. But the noses were transparent. The right-hand light was fogged and all three drew together at the bottom. When he looked down at the rock he was seeing the surface over the scrubby hedge of his unshaven upper lip. The window was surrounded by inscrutable darkness which extended throughout his body. He leaned forward to peer round the window-frame but it went with him. He altered the frame for a moment with a frown. He turned the three lights right round the horizon. He spoke, frowning.

"That is the ordinary experience of living. There is nothing strange in that." He shook his head and busied himself. He turned the windows on his own body and examined the skin critically. Great patches were pink over the scars and he cried out.

"Sunburn!"

He grabbed his vest and pulled it on. The material was so nearly dry that he accepted it as such and shuffled into his pants. The luminous windows became the ordinary way of seeing. He gathered his papers, put them in the identity book and stowed the whole packet in the pocket of his reefer. He padded round the top of the rock, handling his clothes and testing them for dryness. They did not feel damp so much as heavy. There was no moisture that would come off on the fingers or could be wrung out, but where he lifted them from the rock they left their shapes in darker stone that faded slowly in the sun.

He spoke flatly against the blotting-paper.

"I wish I'd kept my seaboots."

He came to his oilskin and knelt, looking at it. Then suddenly he was rummaging through the forgotten pockets. He drew out a sou'wester from which the water ran, and a sodden balaclava. He unfolded the sou'wester and wrung out the balaclava. He spread them and dived at the other pocket. An expression of anxious concentration settled on his face. He fumbled and drew out a greening ha'penny, some string and the crumpled wrapping from a bar of chocolate. He unfolded the paper with great care; but there was nothing left inside. He put his face close to the glittering paper and squinted at it. In one crease there was a single brown grain. He put out his tongue and took the grain. The chocolate stung with a piercing sweetness, momentary and agonizing, and was gone.

He leaned back against the stone dwarf, reached for his socks and pulled them on. He took his seaboot stockings, rolled down the tops and made do with them for boots.

He let his head lie against the dwarf and closed his eyes.

86

The sun shone over his shoulder and the water washed. Inside his head the busy scenes flickered and voices spoke. He experienced all the concomitants of drowsiness but still there did not come the fall and gap of sleep. The thing in the middle of the globe was active and tireless.

"I should like a bed with sheets. I should like a pint or two and a hot meal. I should like a hot bath."

He sat for a while, silent, while the thing jumped from thought to thought. He remembered that speech was proof of identity and his lips began to move again.

"So long as I can want these things without finding the absence of them unendurable; so long as I can tell myself that I am alone on a rock in the middle of the Atlantic and that I have to fight to survive—then I can manage. After all, I am safe compared with those silly sods in H.M. ships. They never know when they're going to be blown up. But I should like to see the brick that could shift this rock."

The thing that could not examine itself danced on in the world behind the eyes.

"And anyway I must not sleep in the daytime. Save that for the miserable nights."

He stood up suddenly and looked round the horizon.

"Dress and eat. Dress for dinner."

He kicked off the seaboot stockings and got into his clothes, all but the duffle and oilskin. He pulled the stockings up over his trousers to the knees. He stood and became voluble in the flat air.

"I call this place the Look-out. That is the Dwarf. The

rock out there under the sun where I came swimming is Safety Rock. The place where I get mussels and stuff is Food Cliff. Where I eat them is—The Red Lion. On the south side where the strap-weed is, I call Prospect Cliff. This cliff here to the west with the funnel in it is——"

He paused, searching for a name. A sea-gull came swinging in under the sun, saw the two figures standing on the Look-out, screamed, side-slipped crazily and wheeled away. It came straight back but at a lower level on his right hand and vanished into the cliff. He edged forward and looked down. There was a sheer, almost unbroken descent on the left and then the cleft in the middle of the cliff, and above that, the funnel. To the right the foot of the cliff was hidden for the highest corner of the Look-out leaned out. He went on hands and knees to the edge and looked down. The cliff was visible for a yard and then turned in and hid itself. The rock began again near the bottom and he could see a glint of feather.

"A lump has fallen out of the cliff."

He searched the water carefully and thought he could make out a square shape deep under the surface. He backed away and stood up.

"Gull Cliff."

The horizon was still empty.

He climbed down the rock to the Red Lion.

"I wish I could remember the name of the whole rock. The Captain said it was a near miss and he laughed. I have it on the tip of my tongue. And I must have a name for this habitual clamber of mine between the Look-out and the Red Lion. I shall call it the High Street."

He saw that the rock on which he sat was dark and glanced over his shoulder. The sun was just leaving him, going down behind the Dwarf, so that the piled stones had become a giant. He got up quickly and lowered himself down the plastered Food Cliff. He hung spreadeagled, traversed a couple of yards and twisted out mussels. The deep sea tide was up now and he had much less scope. He had to lean down and work the mussels loose under water. He climbed back to the Red Lion and began to eat. The great shape of the rock had lost detail and become a blotch against the evening sky. The shadow loomed, vast as a mountain peak. He looked the other way and there were the three rocks diminishing into a dark sea.

"I name you three rocks—Oxford Circus, Piccadilly and Leicester Square."

He went to the dark water-hole and pulled himself in. A little light still came from the hole in the jumbled stones at the other end and when he drank he could see ripples faintly but the red coils were invisible. He put his forefinger straight down into the water and felt the slimy bottom. He lay very still.

"It will rain again."

Then he was jumping and shuddering for there was someone else in the hole with him. Or there was a voice that spoke almost with his, from the water and the slab. As his heart eased he could think coherently of the sound as a rare and forgotten thing, a resonance, an echo. Then immediately he could reason that his voice was full-sized in here so he quietened his body and spoke deliberately.

"Plenty of identity in here, Ladies and Gentlemen——"

He cut his voice off sharply and heard the rock say, "—men——"

"It will rain."

"—ain."

"How are you?"

"—u?"

"I am busy surviving. I am netting down this rock with names and taming it. Some people would be incapable of understanding the importance of that. What is given a name is given a seal, a chain. If this rock tries to adapt me to its ways I will refuse and adapt it to mine. I will impose my routine on it, my geography. I will tie it down with names. If it tries to annihilate me with blotting-paper, then I will speak in here where my words resound and significant sounds assure me of my own identity. I will trap rainwater and add it to this pool. I will use my brain as a delicate machine-tool to produce the results I want. Comfort. Safety. Rescue. Therefore to-morrow I declare to be a thinking day."

He backed out of the water-hole, climbed the High Street and stood on the Look-out by the Dwarf. He dressed in everything, pulled on the damp balaclava and drew the sou'wester round his head with the chinstay down. He looked quickly round the horizon, listened to the faint movement from the invisible aery half-way down

90

Gull Cliff. He went down the High Street, came to his crevice. He sat on the wall by the crevice, put his feet in the grey sweater and wrapped it round them. He got down and wormed his way into the crevice, pushing down his duffle and oilskin. He blew the lifebelt up tight and tied the two breast ends of the tube together with the tape. The lifebelt made a pillow big enough for his head and very soft. He lay on his back and rested his head in the sou'wester on the soft pillow. He inched his arms down on either side of him in the crevice. He spoke to the sky.

"I must dry seaweed and line this crevice. I could be as snug as a bug in a rug."

He shut his eyes.

"Relax each muscle in turn."

Sleep is a condition to be attained by thought like any other.

"The trouble with keeping house on a rock is that there's so much to do. But I shan't get bored, that's one thing."

Relax the muscles of the feet.

"And what a story! A week on a rock. Lectures——"

How to Survive. By Lieutenant—but why not Lieutenant-Commander? Or Commander? Brass Hat and all.

"You men must remember——"

His eyes fell open.

"And I never remembered! Never thought of it! Haven't had a crap for a week!" Or not since before I was blown off

91

the bloody bridge anyway.

The flaps of his sou'wester prevented him from hearing the flatness of his voice against the sky. He lay and meditated the sluggishness of his bowels. This created pictures of chrome and porcelain and attendant circumstances. He put the toothbrush back, and stood, looking at his face in the mirror. The whole business of eating was peculiarly significant. They made a ritual of it on every level, the Fascists as a punishment, the religious as a rite, the cannibal either as a ritual or as a medicine or as a superbly direct declaration to conquest. Killed and eaten. And of course eating with the mouth was only the gross expression of what was a universal process. You could eat with your cock or with your fists, or with your voice. You could eat with hobnailed boots or buying and selling or marrying and begetting or cuckolding——

Cuckolding reminded him. He turned from the mirror, bound his dressing-gown with the cord and opened the bathroom door. And there, coming towards him, as if the rather antiquated expression had conjured him up was Alfred. But it was a different Alfred, pale, sweating, trembling, coming at a run toward. He took the wrist as the fist came at his chest and twisted it till Alfred was gritting his teeth and hissing through them. Secure in his knowledge of the cosmic nature of eating he grinned down at him.

"Hullo, Alfred!"

"You bloody swine!"

"Nosey little man."

"Who've you got in there? Tell me!"

"Now, now. Come along quietly Alfred, we don't want any fuss."

"Don't pretend it's someone else! You bastard! Oh Christ——"

They were by the closed door. Alfred was crying into the lines round his mouth and struggling to get at the door handle.

"Tell me who she is, Chris. I *must* know—for God's sake!"

"Don't ham it, Alfred."

"And don't pretend it's not Sybil, you dirty, thieving bastard!"

"Like to look, Alfred?"

Hiccups. Weak struggles.

"You mean it's someone else? You're not fooling Chris, honestly?"

"Anything to cheer you up old man. Look."

The door opening; Sybil, giving a tiny shriek and pulling the sheet up to her mouth as if this were a bedroom-farce which, of course, in every sense, it was.

"Honestly, Alfred old man, anyone would think you'd married the girl."

But there was a connection between eating and the Chinese box. What was a Chinese box? A coffin? Or those carved ivory ornaments, one inside the other? Yet there was a Chinese box in it somewhere——

Astonished, he lay like a stone man, open-mouthed and

gazing into the sky. The furious struggle against his chest, the slobbering sobs of the weak mouth were still calling their reactions out of his stronger body when he was back in the crevice.

He cleared his throat and spoke aloud.

"Where the hell am I? Where was I?"

He heaved over and lay face downwards in the crevice, his cheeks on the lifebelt.

"Can't sleep."

But sleep is necessary. Lack of sleep was what sent people crazy. He spoke aloud and the lifebelt wobbled under his jaw.

"I was asleep then. I was dreaming about Alfred and Sybil. Go to sleep again."

He lay still and considered sleep. But it was a tantalizingly evasive subject.

Think about women then or eating. Think about eating women, eating men, crunching up Alfred, that other girl, that boy, that crude and unsatisfactory experiment, lie restful as a log and consider the gnawed tunnel of life right up to this uneasy intermission.

This rock.

"I shall call those three rocks out there the Teeth."

All at once he was gripping the lifebelt with both hands and tensing his muscles to defeat the deep shudders that were sweeping through him.

"No! Not the Teeth!"

The teeth were here, inside his mouth. He felt them

with his tongue, the double barrier of bone, each known and individual except the gaps—and there they persisted as a memory if one troubled to think. But to lie on a row of teeth in the middle of the sea——

He began to think desperately about sleep.

Sleep is a relaxation of the conscious guard, the sorter. Sleep is when all the unsorted stuff comes flying out as from a dustbin upset in a high wind. In sleep time was divorced from the straight line so that Alfred and Sybil were on the rock with him and that boy with his snivelling, blubbered face. Or sleep was a consenting to die, to go into complete unconsciousness, the personality defeated, acknowledging too frankly what is implicit in mortality that we are temporary structures patched up and unable to stand the pace without a daily respite from what we most think ours——

"Then why can't I sleep?"

Sleep is where we touch what is better left unexamined. There, the whole of life is bundled up, dwindled. There the carefully hoarded and enjoyed personality, our only treasure and at the same time our only defence must die into the ultimate truth of things, the black lightning that splits and destroys all, the positive, unquestionable nothingness.

And I lie here, a creature armoured in oilskin, thrust into a crack, a morsel of food on the teeth that a world's lifetime has blunted.

Oh God! Why can't I sleep?

Gripping the lifebelt in two hands, with face lifted,

eyes staring straight ahead down the gloomy tunnel, he whispered the answer to his own question in a mixture of astonishment and terror.

"I am afraid to."

7

The light changed before the staring eyes but so slowly that they did not notice any difference. They looked, rather, at the jumble of unsorted pictures that presented themselves at random. There was still the silent, indisputable creature that sat at the centre of things, but it seemed to have lost the knack of distinguishing between pictures and reality. Occasionally the gate in the lower part of the globe would open against the soft lifebelt and words come out, but each statement was so separated by the glossy and illuminated scenes the creature took part in that it did not know which was relevant to which.

"I said that I should be sick."

"Drink. Food. Sanity. Rescue."

"I shall call them the——"

But the glossy images persisted, changed, not as one cloud shape into another but with sudden and complete differences of time and place.

"Sit down, Martin."

"Sir."

"We're considering whether we should recommend you

for a commission. Cigarette?"

"Thank you, sir."

Sudden smile over the clicked lighter.

"Got your nickname on the lower deck yet?"

Smile in return, charming, diffident.

"'Fraid so, sir. Inevitably, I believe."

"Like Dusty Miller and Nobby Clark."

"Yes, sir."

"How's the life up forrard?"

"It's—endurable, sir."

"We want men of education and intelligence; but most of all, men of character. Why did you join the Navy?"

"One felt one ought to—well, help, sir, if you see what I mean?"

Pause.

"I see you're an actor in civvy street."

Careful.

"Yes, sir. Not a terribly good one, I'm afraid."

"Author?"

"Nothing much, yet, sir."

"What would you have liked to be then?"

"One felt it was—unreal. Not like this. You know, sir! Here in this ship. Here we *are* getting down to the basic business of life—something worth doing. I wish I'd been a sailor."

Pause.

"Why would you like a commission, Martin?"

"As an ordinary seaman, sir, one's the minutest cog in a

98

machine. As an officer one would have more chance of hitting the old Hun for six, sir, actually."

Pause.

"Did you volunteer, Martin?"

He's got it all on those papers there if he chooses to look it up.

Frank.

"Actually, no sir."

He's blushing, under that standard Dartmouth mask of his.

"That will be all, Martin, thank you."

"Aye, aye, sir, thank you, sir."

He's blushing like a virgin of sixteen.

"She's the producer's wife, old man, here where are you going?"

An exceptionally small French dictionary, looking like an exceptionally large red eraser.

A black lacquer cash-box on which the gilt was worn.

The Chinese box was evasive. Sometimes it was the fretted ivories, one inside the other, sometimes it was a single box like a cash-box. But however evasive, it was important and intrusive.

She's the producer's wife, old man. Fat. White. Like a maggot with tiny black eyes. I should like to eat you.

I should love to play Danny. I should love to eat you. I should love to put you in a play. How can I put you anywhere if I haven't eaten you? He's a queer. He'd love to eat you. And I should love to eat you too. You're not a person, my sweet, you're an instrument of pleasure.

A Chinese box.

A sword is a phallus. What a huge mountain-shaking joke! A phallus is a sword. Down, dog, down. Down on all fours where you belong.

Then he was looking at a half-face and crying out. The half-face belonged to one of the feathered reptiles. The creature was perched on the slab and looking down sideways at him. As he cried out the wide wings beat and flapped away and immediately a glossy picture swept the blue sky and the stone out of sight. This was a bright patch, sometimes like a figure eight lying on its side and sometimes a circle. The circle was filled with blue sea where gulls were wheeling and settling and loving to eat and fight. He felt the swing of the ship under him, sensed the bleak stillness and silence that settled on the bridge as the destroyer slid by the thing floating in the water—a thing, humble and abused and still, among the fighting beaks, an instrument of pleasure.

He struggled out into the sun, stood up and cried flatly in the great air.

"I am awake!"

Dense blue with white flecks and diamond flashes.

Foam, flowering abundantly round the three rocks.

He turned away from the night.

"Today is a thinking day."

He undressed quickly to his trousers and sweater, spread his clothing in the sun and went down to the Red Lion. The tide was so low that mussels were in sight by the ship load.

Mussels were food but one soon tired of them. He wondered for a moment whether he should collect some sweets but his stomach did not entertain the idea. He thought of chocolate instead and the silver paper came into his mind. He sat there, chewing mechanically while his mind's eye watched silver, flashing bright.

"After all, I may be rescued today."

He examined the thought and found that the whole idea was neutral as the mussels had become, harsh and negative as the fresh water. He climbed to the water-hole and crawled in. The red deposit lay in a band nearly two inches wide at the nearer edge.

He cried out in the echoing hole.

"It will rain again!"

Proof of identity.

"I must measure this pool. I must ration myself. I must force water to come to me if necessary. I must have water."

A well. Boring through rock. A dew pond. Line with clay and straw. Precipitation. Education. Intelligence.

He reached out his hand and prodded down with the finger. When his hand had submerged to the knuckles his finger-tip met slime and slid. Then rock. He took a deep breath. There was darker water farther on under the window.

"A fool would waste water by crawling forward, washing this end about just to see how much there is left. But I won't. I'll wait and crawl forward as the water shrinks. And before that there will be rain."

He went quickly to his clothes, took out the silver paper and the string and climbed back to the Dwarf.

He frowned at the Dwarf and began to talk into the blotting-paper.

"East or west is useless. If convoys appear in either of those quarters they would be moving towards the rock anyway. But they may appear to the south, or less likely, to the north. But the sun does not shine from the north. South is the best bet, then."

He took the Dwarf's head off and laid the stone carefully on the Look-out. He knelt down and smoothed the silver paper until the sheet gleamed under his hand. He forced the foil to lie smoothly against the head and bound it in place with the string. He put the silver head back on the Dwarf, went to the southern end of the Look-out and stared at the blank face. The sun bounced at him from the paper. He bent his knees until he was looking into the paper at eye-level and still he saw a distorted sun. He shuffled round in such arc as the southern end of the Look-out would allow and still he saw the sun. He took the silver head off the Dwarf again, polished the silver on

102

his seaboot stockings and put it back. The sun winked at him. There stood on the Look-out a veritable man and one who carried a flashing signal on his shoulders.

"I shall be rescued today."

He fortified and deepened the meaningless statement with three steps of a dance but stopped with a grimace.

"My feet!"

He sat down and leaned against the Dwarf on the south side.

Today is a thinking day.

"I haven't done so badly."

He altered the arch over his window with a frown.

"Ideally of course, the stone should be a sphere. Then no matter where the ship appears in an arc of one hundred and eighty degrees the sun will bounce straight at her from the Dwarf. If a ship is under the horizon then the gleam might fetch her crow's-nest, following it along like a hand of arrest on the shoulder, persisting, nagging, till even the dullest of seamen would notice and the idea sink in."

The horizon remained empty.

"I must get a sphere. Perhaps I could beat the nearest to it with another stone until it rounds. Stone mason as well. Who was it cut stone cannon-balls? Michael Angelo? But I must look for a very round stone. Never a dull moment. Just like Itma."

He got up and went down to the sea. He peered over the edge of the little cliff by the mussels but saw nothing worth having. There was green weed and a mass of stone between him and the three rocks but he turned away from it. He went instead to Prospect Cliff, climbed down the ledges to low water. But here there was nothing but masses of weed that stank. His climb tired him and he clung over the water for a moment, searching the surface of the rock with his eyes for anything of value. There was a coralline substance close to his face, thin and pink like icing and then not pink as though it were for ever changing its mind to purple. He stroked the smooth stuff with one finger. They called that paint Barmaid's Blush and splashed on gallons with the inexpert and casual hand of the wartime sailor. The colour was supposed to merge a ship into the sea and air at the perilous hour of dawn. There were interminable hard acres of the pink round scuttles and on gun shields, whole fields on sides and top hamper, hanging round the hard angles, the utilitarian curves, the grudgingly conceded living quarters of ships on the Northern Patrol, like pink icing or the coral growths on a washed rock. He took his face away from the casing and turned to climb the ladders to the bridge. There must be acres of the stuff spread on the child-time rocks at Tresellyn. That was where Nat had taken her—taken her in two senses, grateful for the tip.

The ship rolled heavily and here was Nat descending the upper ladder like a daddy-longlegs, carefully placing the remote ends of the limbs for security and now faced with a crisis at the sight of the face and the cap. Here is Nat saluting as ever off balance, but this time held in position by one arm and two legs.

"Wotcher, Nat. Happy in your work?"

Dutiful Nat-smile though a little queasy. See the bright side.

"Yes, sir."

Amble aft you drawn-out bastard.

Climb, climb. The bridge, a little wind and afternoon.

"Hallo. Mean course o-nine-o. Now on zag at one-one-o. And I may say, dead in station, not wandering all over the ocean the way you leave her. She's all yours and the Old Man is in one of his moods, so watch out for sparks."

"Zig coming up in ten seconds? I've got her."

"See you again at the witching hour."

"Port fifteen. Midships. Steady."

He looked briefly round the convoy and then aft. Nat was there, tediously in his usual place, legs wide apart, face in hands. The corticened deck lurched under him, re-arranged itself and he swayed on the rail. The luminous window that looked down at him bent at the sides in a snarl that was disguised as a grin.

Christ, how I hate you. I could eat you. Because you fathomed her mystery, you have a right to handle her transmuted cheap tweed; because you both have made a place where I can't get; because in your fool innocence you've got what I had to get or go mad.

Then he found himself additionally furious with Nath-aniel, not because of Mary, not because he had happened on her as he might have tripped over a ring-bolt but because he dared sit so, tilting with the sea, held by a thread, so near the end that would be at once so anguishing and restful like the bursting of a boil.

"Christ!"

Wildebeeste had turned seconds ago.

"Starboard thirty! Half-ahead together!"

Already, from the apex of the destroyer screen, a light was stabbing erratically.

"Midships! Steady. Slow ahead together."

There was a clatter from the ladder. The Captain burst at him.

"What the bloody hell are you playing at?"

Hurried and smooth.

"I thought there was wreckage on the starboard bow, sir, and couldn't be sure so I maintained course and speed till we were clear, sir."

The Captain stopped, one hand on the screen of the bridge and lowered at him.

"What sort of wreckage?"

"Baulks of timber, sir, floating just under the surface."

"Starboard look-out!"

"Sir?"

"Did you see any wreckage?"

"No, sir."

"—I may have been mistaken, sir, but I judged it better to make sure, sir."

The Captain bored in, face to face so that his grip on the rock tightened as he remembered. The Captain's face was

big, pale and lined, the eyes red-rimmed with sleepless-
ness and gin. It examined for a moment what the window
had to exhibit. The two shadowy noses on either side of
the window caught a faint, sweet scent. Then the face
changed, not dramatically, not registering, not making ob-
vious, but changing like a Nat-face, from within. Under
the pallor and moist creases, in the corners of the mouth
and eyes, came the slight muscular shift of complicated
tensions till the face was rearranged and bore like an open
insult, the pattern of contempt and disbelief.

The mouth opened.

"Carry on."

In a confusion too complete for answer or salute he
watched the face turn away and take its understanding
and contempt down the ladder.

There was heat and blood.

"Signal, sir, from Captain D. 'Where are you going to
my pretty maid?'"

Signalman with a wooden face. Heat and blood.

"Take it to the Captain."

"Aye aye, sir."

He turned back to the binnacle.

"Port fifteen. Midships. Steady."

Looking under his arm he saw Nathaniel pass the
bridge messenger in the waist. Seen thus, he was a bat
hanging upside down from the roof of a cave. Nat passed
on, walking and lurching till the break of the fo'castle hid
him.

He found he was cursing an invisible Nat, cursing him for Mary, for the contempt in old Gin-soak's face. The centre, looking in this reversed world over the binnacle, found itself beset by a storm of emotions, acid and inky and cruel. There was a desperate amazement that anyone so good as Nat, so unwillingly loved for the face that was always rearranged from within, for the serious attention, for love given without thought, should also be so quiveringly hated as though he were the only enemy. There was amazement that to love and to hate were now one thing and one emotion. Or perhaps they could be separated. Hate was as hate had always been, an acid, the corroding venom of which could be borne only because the hater was strong.

"I am a good hater."

He looked quickly at the deck watch, across at *Wildebeeste* and gave orders for the new course.

And love? Love for Nat? That was this sorrow dissolved through the hate so that the new solution was a deadly thing in the chest and the bowels.

He muttered over the binnacle.

"If I were that glass toy that I used to play with I could float in a bottle of acid. Nothing could touch me then."

Zag.

"That's what it is. Ever since I met her and she interrupted the pattern coming at random, obeying no law of life, facing me with the insoluble, unbearable problem of her existence the acid's been chewing at my guts. I can't even kill her because that would be her final victory over me. Yet as long as she lives the acid will eat. She's there. In the flesh. In the not even lovely flesh. In the cheap mind. Obsession. Not love. Or if love, insanely compounded of this jealousy of her very being. *Odi et amo*. Like that thing I tried to write."

There were lace curtains in decorous curves either side of the oak occasional table with its dusty fern. The round table in the centre of the almost unused parlour smelt of polish—might one day support a coffin in state, but until then, nothing. He looked round at the ornaments and plush, took a breath of the air that was trapped this side of the window, smelt of last year and varnish like the vilest cooking sherry. The room would suit her. She would fit it, she was the room at all points except for the mania.

He looked down at the writing-pad on his knee.

Zig.

"And that wasn't the half of it. And the acid still eats. Who could ever dream that he would fall in love—or be trapped—by a front parlour on two feet?"

He began to pace backward and forward on the bridge.

"As long as she lives the acid will eat. There's nothing that can stand that. And killing her would make it worse."

He stopped. Looked back along the deck at the quarter-deck and the empty, starboard rail.

"Christ! Starboard twenty——"

There was a sense in which she could be—or say that the acid flow could be checked. Not to pass Petty Officer

Roberts' message on was one thing—but that merely ac-
quiesced in the pattern. But say one nudged circumstances
—not in the sense that one throttled with the hands or
fired a gun—but gently shepherded them the way they
might go? Since it would be a suggestion to circumstances
only it could not be considered what a strict moralist
might call it——

"And who cares anyway?"

This was to run with a rapier at the arras without more
than a hope of success.

"He may never sit there again."

Then the officer of the watch in the execution of his
duty gives a helm order to avoid floating wreckage or a
drifting mine and no one is any the worse.

"But if he sits there again——"

The corrosive swamped him. A voice cried out in his
belly—I do not want him to die! The sorrow and hate bit
deep, went on biting. He cried out with his proper voice.

"Does no one understand how I feel?"

The look-outs had turned on their perches. He scowled
at them and felt another warmth in his face. His voice
came out savagely.

"Get back to your sectors."

He leaned over the binnacle and felt how his body
shook.

"I am chasing after—a kind of peace."

Barmaid's blush with hair that was coarse even for a
barmaid. He looked at the ledges of rock.

"A kind of peace."

Coral growth.

He shook his head as though he were shaking water out of his hair.

"I came down here for something."

But there was nothing, only weed and rock and water.

He climbed back to the Red Lion, gathered some of the uneaten mussels that he had left from the morning and went up the High Street to the Look-out. He sat under the south side of the winking Dwarf and opened them with his knife. He ate with long pauses between each mouthful. When he had finished the last one he lay back.

"Christ."

They were no different from the mussels of yesterday but they tasted of decay.

"Perhaps I left them too long in the sun."

But they hang in the sun between tides for hours!

"How many days have I been here?"

He thought fiercely, then made three scratches on the rock with his knife.

"I must not let anything escape that would reinforce personality. I must make decisions and carry them out. I have put a silver head on the Dwarf. I have decided not to be tricked into messing about with the water-hole. How far away is the horizon? Five miles? I could see a crow's-nest at ten miles. I can advertise myself over a circle twenty miles in diameter. That's not bad.

111

The Atlantic is about two thousand miles wide up here. Twenty into two thousand goes a hundred."

He knelt down and measured off a line ten inches in length as near as he could judge.

"That makes it a tenth of an inch."

He put the blade of his knife on the line at about two inches from the end and rotated the haft slowly till the point made a white mark in the grey rock. He squatted back on his heels and looked at the diagram.

"With a really big ship I could be seen at fifteen miles."

He put the point of the knife back on the mark and enlarged it. He paused, then went on scraping till the mark was the size of a silver threepenny-bit. He put out his foot and scuffed the seaboot stocking over the mark until it was grey and might have been there since the rock was made.

"I shall be rescued today."

He stood up and looked into the silver face. The sun was still shining back at him. He traced mental lines from the sun to the stone, bounced them out at this part of the horizon and that. He went close to the Dwarf and looked down at the head to see if he could find his face reflected there. The sunlight bounced up in his eyes. He jerked upright.

"The air! You fool! You clot! They ferry planes and they must use this place for checking the course—and Coastal Command, looking for U-boats——"

He cupped his hands at his eyes and turned slowly

round, looking at the sky. The air was dense blue and interrupted by nothing but the sun over the south sea. He flung his hands away and began to walk hastily up and down by the Look-out.

"A thinking day."

The Dwarf was all right for ships—they were looking across at a silhouette. They would see the Dwarf or perhaps the gleam of the head. But to a plane, the Dwarf would be invisible, merged against the rock, and the glint from the silver might be a stray crystal of quartz. There was nothing about the rock to catch the eye. They might circle at a few thousand feet—a mile, two miles—and see nothing that was different. From above, the stone would be a tiny grey patch, that was eye-catching only by the surf that spread round in the sea.

He looked quickly and desperately up, then away at the water.

A pattern.

Men make patterns and superimpose them on nature. At ten thousand feet the rock would be a pebble; but suppose the pebble were striped? He looked at the trenches. The pebble was striped already. The upended layers would be grey with darker lines of trench between them.

He held his head in his hands.

A chequer. Stripes. Words. S.O.S.

"I cannot give up my clothes. Without them I should freeze to death. Besides if I spread them out they would still be less visible than this guano."

He looked down the High Street between his hands.

"Pare away here and here and there. Make all smooth. Cut into a huge, shadowed S.O.S."

He dropped his hands and grinned.

"Be your age."

He squatted down again and considered in turn the material he had with him. Cloth. Small sheets of paper. A rubber lifebelt.

Seaweed.

He paused, lifted his hands and cried out in triumph.

"Seaweed!"

8

There were tons of the stuff hanging round the rock, floating or coiled down under water by Prospect Cliff.

"Men make patterns."

Seaweed, to impose an unnatural pattern on nature,
a pattern that would cry out to any rational beholder
—Look! Here is thought. Here is man!

"The best form would be a single indisputable line
drawn at right angles to the trenches, piled so high that
it will not only show a change of colour but even throw a
shadow of its own. I must make it at least a yard wide and
it must be geometrically straight. Later I will fill up one
of the trenches and turn the upright into a cross. Then the
rock will become a hot cross bun."

Looking down towards the three Rocks he planned the
line to descend across the trenches, parallel more or less
to the High Street. The line would start at the Red Lion
and come up to the Dwarf. It would be an operation.

He went quickly down the High Street: and now that
he had found a job with point, he was muttering without
knowing why.

"Hurry! Hurry!"

Then his ears began to fill with the phantom buzzing of planes. He kept looking up and fell once, cutting himself. Only when he was already pulling at the frondy weed by Food Cliff did he pause.

"Don't be a fool. Take it easy. There's no point in looking up because you can do nothing to attract attention. Only a clot would go dancing and waving his shirt because he thought there was a plane about five miles up."

He craned back his head and searched the sky but found nothing besides blueness and sun. He held his breath and listened and heard nothing but the inner, mingled humming of his own life, nothing outside but the lap and gurgle of water. He straightened his neck and stood there thinking. He went back to the crevice. He stripped naked and spread his clothing in the sun. He arranged each item carefully to one side of where the line of seaweed would lie. He went back to the Red Lion and looked down at the space between the Red Lion and the three rocks. He turned round and lowered himself over the edge. The water was colder than he remembered, colder than the fresh water that he drank. He ground his teeth and forced himself down and the rock was so sharp against his knees that he reopened the wounds of the first day. His waist was on the rock between his hands and he was groaning. He could not feel bottom and the weed round his calves was colder than the water. The cold squeezed as the water had done in the open sea, so that he was panic-stricken

116

at the memory. He made a high, despairing sound, pushed himself clear of the rock and fell. The water took him with a freezing hand. He opened his eyes and weed was lashing before them. His head broke the surface and he struck out frantically for the rock. He hung there, shivering.

"Take a grip."

There was whiteness under the weed. He pushed off and let his feet sink. Under the weed, caught between his own rock and the three others were boulders, quartz perhaps, stacked and unguessable. He stood, crouched in the water, half-supporting his weight with swimming movements of the arms and felt round him with his feet. Carefully he found foothold and stood up. The water reached to his chest and the weed dragged at him. He took a breath and ducked. He seized weed and tried to tear off fronds but they were very tough and he could win no more than a handful before he had to surface again. He began to collect weed without ducking, reaping the last foot of the crop. Sometimes when he pulled there would be a stony turn and slight shock, or the water-slowed movements of re-adjustment. He threw weed up on the rock and the fronds flopped down over the edge, dripping.

Suddenly the weed between his feet tugged and something brushed over his toes. A line of swift and erratic movement appeared in the weed, ceased. He clawed at the cliff and hung there, drawing his legs up.

The water lapped.

"Crab. Lobster."

He kneed his painful way to the Red Lion and lay down by the weed till his heart steadied.

"I loathe it."

He crawled to the edge of the cliff and looked down. At once, as if his eye had created it, he saw the lobster among the weed, different in dragon-shape, different in colour. He knelt, looking down, mesmerized while the worms of loathing crawled over his skin.

"Beast. Filthy sea-beast."

He picked up a mussel shell and threw it with all his strength into the water. At the smack, the lobster clenched like a fist and was gone.

"That line of seaweed's going to take a devil of a time to build."

He shook himself free of the worms on his skin. He lowered himself over Prospect Cliff. The bottom four or five feet was covered with a hanging mass of strap-weed. At the surface of the water, weed floated out so that the sea seemed solid.

"Low water."

He climbed along the rock and began to tug at the weed but it would not come off. The roots clung to the rock with suckers more difficult to remove than limpets or mussels. Some of the weeds were great bushes that ended in dimpled bags full of jelly. Others were long swords but with a fluted and wavered surface and edge. The rest was smooth brown leather like an assembly of sword belts for all the officers in the world. Under the weed the rock was furry with coloured growths or hard and decorative with stuff that looked like uncooked batter. There was also Barmaid's Blush. There were tiny bubblings and pips and splashes.

He tugged at a bunch of weed with one hand while he hung on to the rock with the other. He cursed and climbed back up the rock, walked up the High Street to the Lookout and stood looking at the sea and sky.

He came to with a jump.

"Don't waste time. Be quick."

He went to the crevice, slung the knife round his neck by its lanyard and picked up the lifebelt. He unscrewed the mouth of the tit, let the air out and climbed down the rock. He slung the lifebelt over his arm and went at the weed-roots with the knife. They were not only hard as hard rubber but slippery. He had to find a particular angle and a particular careful sobriety of approach before he could get the edge of his knife into them. He wore the weed like firewood over his shoulder. He held the lifebelt in his teeth and drew fronds of weed through between the lifebelt and the tape. He reversed his position, holding on with his left arm and gathering with his right. The weed made a great bundle on his shoulder that draped down and fell past his knees in a long, brown smear.

He climbed to the Red Lion, and flung down the weed. At a distance of a few feet from him it looked like a small patch. He laid out the separate blades, defining the straight line that would interrupt the trenches. In the trenches themselves the weed had no support.

119

"I must fill the trenches flush with the wall where the weed crosses them."

When he had used up all the weed the load stretched from the Red Lion to the Look-out. On the average the line was two inches wide.

He went back to Prospect Cliff and got more weed. He squatted in the Red Lion with his forehead corrugated. He shut one eye and considered his handiwork. The line was hardly visible. He climbed round to the cliff again.

There was a sudden plop in the water by the farthest of the three rocks, so that he sprang round. Nothing. No foam, only a dimpled interruption in the pattern of wavelets.

"I ought to catch fish."

He gathered himself another load of weed. The jellied bags burst when he pressed them, and he put one of the bags to his lips but the taste was neutral. He carried another load to the Red Lion and another. When he piled the weed in the first trench it did not come within a foot of the top.

He stood in the trench, looking down at the red and brown weed and felt suddenly listless.

"Twelve loads? Twenty? And then the line to thicken after that——"

Intelligence sees so clearly what is to be done and can count the cost beforehand.

"I will rest for a while."

He went to the Dwarf and sat down under the empty sky. The seaweed stretched away across the rock like a trail.

"Harder than ever in my life before. Worn out for to-day."

He put his head on his knees and muttered to the ghost of a diagram—a line with a grey blob on it.

"I haven't had a crap since we were torpedoed."

He sat motionless and meditated on his bowels. Presently he looked up. He saw that the sun was on the decline and made a part of the horizon particularly clear and near. Squinting at it he thought he could even see the minute distortions that the waves made in the perfect curve of the world.

There was a white dot sitting between the sun and Safety Rock. He watched closely and saw that the dot was a gull sitting in the water, letting itself drift. All at once he had a waking vision of the gull rising and flying east over the sea's shoulder. To-morrow morning it could be floating among the stacks and shields of the Hebrides or following the plough on some Irish hill-side. As an intense experience that interrupted the bright afternoon before him he saw the ploughman in his cloth cap hitting out at the squawking bird.

"Get away from me now and the bad luck go with you!"

But the bird would not perch on the boundary-stone, open its bill and speak as in all folk lore. Even if it were more than a flying machine it could not pass on news of the scarred man sitting on a rock in the middle of the sea. He got up and began to pace to and fro on the Look-out. He took the thought out and looked at it.

I may never get away from this rock at all.

Speech is identity.

"You are all a machine. I know you, wetness, hardness, movement. You have no mercy but you have no intelligence. I can outwit you. All I have to do is to endure. I breathe this air into my own furnace. I kill and eat. There is nothing to——"

He paused for a moment and watched the gull drifting nearer; but not so near that the reptile under the white was visible.

"There is nothing to fear."

The gull was being carried along by the tide. Of course the tide operated here too, in mid-Atlantic, a great wave that swept round the world. It was so great that it thrust out tongues that became vast ocean currents, sweeping the water in curves that were ten thousand miles long. So there was a current that flowed past this rock, rising, pausing, reversing and flowing back again eternally and pointlessly. The current would continue to do so if life were rubbed off the skin of the world like the bloom off a grape. The rock sat immovable and the tide went sweeping past.

He watched the gull come floating by Prospect Cliff. It preened its feathers and fluttered like a duck in a pond.

He turned abruptly away and went quickly down to Prospect Cliff. Half the hanging seaweed was covered.

To-morrow.

"Exhausted myself. Mustn't overdo it."

Plenty to do on a rock. Never a dull moment.

He considered the mussels with positive distaste and switched his mind instead to the bags of jelly on the seaweed. He had a vague feeling that his stomach was talking to him. It disliked mussels. As for anemones—the bare thought made the bag contract and send a foul taste to his mouth.

"Overwork. Exposure. Sunburn, perhaps. I mustn't overdo it."

He reminded himself seriously that this was the day on which he was going to be rescued but could not rediscover conviction.

"Dress."

He put on his clothes, walked round the Dwarf then sat down again.

"I should like to turn in. But I mustn't as long as there's light. She might come close for a look, blow her siren and go away again if I didn't show myself. But I thought to some purpose today. To-morrow I must finish the seaweed. She may be just below the horizon. Or up so high I can't see her. I must wait."

He hunched down by the Dwarf and waited. But time had infinite resource and what at first had been a purpose became grey and endless and without hope. He began to look for hope in his mind but the warmth had gone or if he found anything it was an intellectual and bloodless ghost.

He muttered.

"I shall be rescued. I shall be rescued."

*

At an end so far from the beginning that he had forgotten everything he had thought while he was there, he lifted his chin and saw that the sun was sinking. He got up heavily, went to the water-hole and drank. The stain of red round the nearer edge was wider.

He echoed.

"I must do something about water."

He dressed as for bed and wrapped the grey sweater round his feet. It made a muffling between them and the rock like the cathedral carpets over stone. That was a particular sensation the feet never found anywhere else particularly when they wore those ridiculous medieval shoes of Michael's all fantasticated but with practically no sole. Beside the acoustics were so bad—wah, wah, wah and then a high whine up among the barrel vault to which one added with every word one spoke as though one were giving a little periodic momentum to a pendulum——

"Can't hear you, old man, not a sausage. Up a bit. Give. I still can't hear you——"

"More? Slower?"

"Not slower for God's sake. Oh, turn it up. That's all for today boys and girls. Wait a bit, Chris. Look, George, Chris isn't coming off here at all——"

"Give him a bit more time, old man. Not your pitch is it, Chris?"

"I can manage, George."

"He'll be better in the other part, old man. Didn't you

see the rehearsal list, Chris? You're doubling—but of course——"

"Helen never said——"

"What's Helen got to do with it?"

"She never said——"

"I make out my own lists, old man."

"Of course, Pete, naturally."

"So you're doubling a shepherd and one of the seven deadly sins, old man. Eh, George, don't you think? Chris for one of the seven deadly sins?"

"Definitely, old man, oh, definitely."

"Well, I do think, Pete, after the amount of work I've done for you, I shouldn't be asked to——"

"Double, old man? Everbody's doubling. I'm doubling. So you're wanted for the seven sins, Chris."

"Which one, Pete?"

"Take your pick, old man. Eh, George? We ought to let dear old Chris pick his favourite sin, don't you, think?"

"Definitely, old boy, definitely."

"Prue's working on them in the crypt, come and look, Chris——"

"But if we've finished until tonight's house——"

"Come along, Chris. The show must go on. Eh, George? You'd like to see which mask Chris thinks would suit him?"

"Well—yes. Yes by God, Pete. I would. After you, Chris."

"I don't think I——"

"After you, Chris."

"Curious feeling to the feet this carpet over stone, George. Something thick and costly, just allowing your senses to feel the basic stuff beneath. There they are Chris, all in a row. What about it?"

"Anything you say, old man."

"What about Pride, George? He could play that without a mask and just stylized make-up, couldn't he?"

"Look, Pete, if I'm doubling I'd sooner not make———"

"Malice, George?"

"Envy, Pete?"

"I don't mind playing Sloth, Pete."

"Not Sloth. Shall we ask Helen, Chris? I value my wife's advice."

"Steady, Pete."

"What about a spot of Lechery?"

"Pete! Stop it."

"Don't mind me Chris, old, man. I'm just a bit wrought-up that's all. Now here's a fine piece of work, ladies and gentleman, guaranteed unworn. Any offers? Going to the smooth-looking gentleman with the wavy hair and profile. Going! Going———"

"What's it supposed to be, old man?"

"Darling, it's simply *you*! Don't you think, George?"

"Definitely, old man, definitely."

"Chris-Greed. Greed-Chris. Know each other."

"Anything to please you, Pete."

"Let me make you two better acquainted. This painted

126

bastard here takes anything he can lay his hands on. Not food, Chris, that's far too simple. He takes the best part, the best seat, the most money, the best notice, the best woman. He was born with his mouth and his flies open and both hands out to grab. He's a cosmic case of the bugger who gets his penny and someone else's bun. Isn't that right, George?"

"Come on, Pete. Come and lie down for a bit."

"Think you can play Martin, Greed?"

"Come on, Pete. He doesn't mean anything, Chris. Just wrought-up. A bit over-excited, eh, Pete?"

"That's all. Yes. Sure. That's all."

"I haven't had a crap for a week."

The dusk came crowding in and the sea-gulls. One sat on the Dwarf and the silver head rocked so that the sea-gull muted and flapped away. He went down to the crevices blew up the lifebelt, tied the tapes and put it under his head. He got his hands tucked in. Then his head felt unprotected, although he was wearing the balaclava, so that he wriggled out and fetched his sou'wester from the Red Lion. He went through the business of insertion again.

"Good God!"

He hauled himself out.

"Where the hell's my oilskin?"

He went scrambling over the rocks to the Red Lion, the water-hole, the Prospect Cliff——

"It can't be by the Dwarf because I never——"

In and out of the trenches, stinking seaweed, clammy, is it underneath?

He found his oilskin where he had left it by the Dwarf. There were white splashes on in. He put his oilskin over his duffle and inserted himself again.

"That's what they can never tell you, never give you any idea. Not the danger or the hardship but the niggling little idiocies, the damnable repetitions, the days dripping away in a scrammy-handed flurry of small mistakes you wouldn't notice if you were at work or could drop into the Red Lion or see your popsie—Where's my knife? Oh, Christ!"

But the knife was present, had swung round and was a rock-like projection under his left ribs. He worked it free and cursed.

"I'd better do my thinking now. I was wrong to do it when I could have worked. If I'd thought last night instead I could have treated the day methodically and done everything.

Now: problems. First I must finish that line of weed. Then I must have a place for clothes so that I never get into a panic again. I'd better stow them here so that I never forget. Second. No third. Clothes were second. First clothes in the crevice, then more weed until the line is finished. Third, water. Can't dig for it. Must catch it when it comes. Choose a trench below guano level and above spray. Make a catchment area."

He worked his lower jaw sideways. His bristles were very uncomfortable in the wool of the balaclava. He could feel the slight freezing, prickling sensation of sunburn on his arms and legs. The unevennesses of the rock were penetrating again.

"It'll soon rain. Then I'll have too much water. What shall I do about this crack? Musn't get my clothes wet. I must rig a tent. Perhaps to-morrow I'll be rescued."

He remembered that he had been certain of rescue in the morning and that made his heart sink unaccountably as though someone had broken his sworn word. He lay, looking up into the stars and wondering if he could find a scrap of wood to touch. But there was no wood on the rock, not even the stub of a pencil. No salt to throw over the left shoulder. Perhaps a splash of sea-water would be just as effective.

He worked his hand down to his right thigh. The old scar must have caught the sun too, for he could feel the raised place burning gently—a not unpleasant feeling but one that took the attention. The bristles in the balaclava made a scratching sound when he grimaced.

"Four. Make the knife sharp enough to shave with. Five. Make sure I'm not egg-bound to-morrow."

The sunburn pricked.

"I am suffering from reaction. I went through hell in the sea and in the funnel, and then I was so pleased to be safe that I went right over the top. And that is fol-lowed by a set-back. I must sleep, must keep quite still and concentrate on the business of sleeping."

The sunburn went on pricking, the bristles scratched and scraped and the unevennesses of the rock lit their slow, smouldering fires. They stayed there like the sea. Even when consciousness was modified they insisted. They became a luminous landscape, they became a universe and he oscillated between moments of hanging in space, observing them and of being extended to every excruciating corner.

He opened his eyes and looked up. He shut them again and muttered to himself.

"I am dreaming."

He opened his eyes and the sunlight stayed there. The light lulled the fires to a certain extent because the mind could at last look away from them. He lay, looking at the daylight sky and trying to remember the quality of this time that had suddenly foreshortened itself.

"I wasn't asleep at all!"

And the mind was very disinclined to hutch out of the crevice and face what must be done. He spoke toneless words into the height of air over him.

"I shall be rescued today."

He hauled himself out of the crevice and the air was warm so that he undressed to trousers and sweater. He folded his clothes carefully and put them in the crevice. When he hutched forward in the water-hole the red deposit made a mark across his chest. He drank a great deal of water and when he stopped drinking he could see that there was a wider space of darkness between the water and the window.

"I must get more water."

He lay still and tried to decide whether it was more important to arrange for catching water or to finish the line of weed. That reminded him how quickly time could pass if you let it out of your sight so he scrambled back to the Look-out. This was a day of colour. The sun burned and the water was deep blue and sparkled gaily. There was colour spilt over the rocks, shadows that were deep purple until you looked straight at them. He peered down the High Street and it was a picture. He shut his eyes and then opened them again but the rock and the sea seemed no more real. They were a pattern of colour that filled the three lights of his window.

"I am still asleep. I am shut inside my body."

He went to the Red Lion and sat by the sea.

"What did I do that for?"

He frowned at the water.

"I mean to get food. But I'm not hungry. I must get weed."

He fetched the lifebelt and knife from the crevice and went to Prospect Cliff. He had to climb farther along the ledges for weed because the nearer part of the cliff was stripped already. He came to a ledge that was vaguely familiar and had to think.

"I came here to get stones for the Dwarf. I tried to

shift that stone there but it wouldn't move although it was cracked."

He frowned at the stone. Then he worked his way down until he was hanging on the cliff by it with both hands and the crack was only a foot from his face. Like all the rest of the cliff where the water could reach it was cemented with layers of barnacles and enigmatic growths. But the crack was wider. The whole stone had moved and skewed perhaps an eighth of an inch. Inside the crack was a terrible darkness.

He stayed there, looking at the loose rock until he forgot what he was thinking. He was envisaging the whole rock as a thing in the water, and he was turning his head from side to side.

"How the hell is it that this rock is so familiar? I've never been here before——"

Familiar, not as a wartime acquaintance whom one knows so quickly because one is forced to live close to him for interminable stretches of hours but familiar as a relative, seldom seen, but to be reckoned with, year after year, familiar as a childhood friend, a nurse, some acquaintance with a touch of eternity behind him; familiar now, as the rocks of childhood, examined and reapprized holiday after holiday, remembered in the darkness of bed, in winter, imagined as a shape one's fingers can feel in the air——

There came a loud plop from the three rocks. He scrambled quickly to the Red Lion but saw nothing.

"I ought to fish."

The seaweed in the trenches stank. There came another plop from the sea and he was in time to see the ripples spreading. He put his hands on either cheek to think but the touch of hair distracted him.

"I must have a beard pretty well. Bristles, anyway. Strange that bristles go on growing even when the rest of you is——"

He went quickly to Prospect Cliff and got a load of weed and dumped it in the nearest trench. He went slowly up the High Street to the Look-out and sat down, his opened hands on either side of him. His head sank between his knees. The lap lap of water round Safety Rock was very quieting and a gull stood on the Look-out like an image.

The sounds of the inside body spread. The vast darkness was full of them as a factory is full of the sound of machinery. His head made a tiny bobbing motion each time his heart beat.

He was jerked out of this state by a harsh scream. The gull had advanced across the rock, its wings half-open, head lowered.

"What do you want?"

The feathered reptile took two steps sideways then shuffled its wings shut. The beak preened under the wing.

"If I had a crap I'd feel better."

He heaved himself round and looked at the Dwarf who winked at him with a silver eye. The line of the horizon was hard and near. Again he thought he could see indentations in the curve.

The trouble was there were no cushions on the rock, no tussocks. He thought for a moment of fetching his duffle and folding the skirt as a seat but the effort seemed too great.

"My flesh aches inside as though it were bruised. The hardness of the rock is wearing out my flesh. I will think about water."

Water was insinuating, soft and yielding.

"I must arrange some kind of shelter. I must arrange to catch water."

He came to a little, felt stronger and worried. He frowned at the tumbled rocks that were so maddeningly and evasively familiar and followed with his eye the thin line of weed. It shone in places. Perhaps the weed would appear from the air as a shining strip.

"I could catch water in my oilskin. I could make the wall of a trench into a catchment area."

He stopped talking and lay back until the unevenness of the Dwarf as a chair-back made him lean forward again. He sat, hunched up and frowning.

"I am aware of——"

He looked up.

"I am aware of a weight. A ponderous squeezing. Agoraphobia or anyway the opposite of claustrophobia. A pressure."

Water catchment.

He got to his feet and climbed back down the High Street. He examined the next trench to his sleeping crevice.

134

"Prevailing wind. I must catch water from an area facing south west."

He took his knife and drew a line sloping down across the leaning wall. It ended in a hollow, set back to the depth of his fist where the wall met the bottom of the trench. He went to the Dwarf, carefully extracted a white potato and brought it back. On the end of the clasp knife was a projection about a quarter of an inch long which was intended as a screwdriver. He placed this against the rock about an inch above the slanting line and tapped the other end of his knife with the stone. The rock came away in thin flakes. He put the screwdriver in the slanting line and tapped till the line sank in. Soon he had made a line perhaps an eighth of an inch deep and a foot long. He went to the bottom end of the line.

"Begin at the most important end of the line. Then no matter how soon the rain comes I can catch some of it."

The noise of the taps was satisfactorily repeated in the trench and he felt enclosed as though he were working in a room.

"I could spread my duffle or oilskin over this trench and then I should have a roof. That ponderous feeling is not so noticeable here. That's partly because I am in a room and partly because I am working."

His arms ached but the line rose away from the floor and he could work in an easier position. He made a dreamy calculation to see whether increasing ease would overtake tiredness and found that it would not. He sat on the floor with his face a few inches from the rock. He leaned his forehead on stone. His hand fell open.

"I could go to the crevice and lie down for a bit. Or I could roll up in my duffle by the Dwarf."

He jerked his head away from the rock and set to work again. The cut part of the line lengthened. This part met the part he had cut first and he sat back to examine it.

"I should have cut it back at a slant. Damn."

He grimaced at the rock and went back over the cut so that the bottom of the groove trended inward.

"Make it deeper near the end."

Because the amount of water in the cut—but he changed his mind and did the calculation out loud.

"The amount of water in any given length of the cut will consist of all the water collected higher up, and also will be proportional to the area of rock above."

He tapped at the rock and the flakes fell. His hands gave out and he sat on the floor of the trench, looking at his work.

"After this I shall do a real engineering job. I shall find a complex area round a possible basin and cut a network of lines that will guide the water to it. That will be rather interesting. Like sand-castles."

Or like Roman emperors, bringing water to the city from the hills.

"This is an aqueduct. I call it the Claudian."

He began to flake again, imposing purpose on the senseless rock.

136

"I wonder how long I've been doing that?"

He lay down in the trench and felt his back bruise. The Claudian was a long, whitish scar.

"There is something venomous about the hardness of this rock. It is harder than rock should be. And—familiar."

The ponderous weight squeezed down. He struggled up to a sitting position.

"I should have dried seaweed and lined the crevice. But there are too many things to do. I need another hand on this job of living and being rescued. Perhaps I could find another place to sleep. In the open? I feel warm enough."

Too warm.

"My flesh is perceptible inside—as though it were bruised everywhere to the bone. And big. Tumescent."

The globe of darkness turned a complicated window towards the sky. The voice evaporated at the gate like escaping steam on a dry day.

"I'm working too hard. If I don't watch out I shall exhaust myself. Anyway I'll hand it to you, Chris. I don't think many people would——"

He stopped suddenly, then began again.

"Chris. Christopher! Christopher Hadley Martin——"

The words dried up.

There was an instrument of examination, a point that knew it existed. There were sounds that came out of the lower part of a face. They had no meaning attached to them. They were useless as tins thrown out with the lids buckled back.

137

"Christopher. Christopher!"

He reached out with both arms as though to grab the words before they dried away. The arms appeared before the window and in complete unreason they filled him with terror.

"Oh, my God."

He wrapped his arms round him, hugged himself close, rocked from side to side. He began to mutter.

"Steady. Steady. Keep calm."

9

He got up and sat gingerly on the side of the trench. He could feel the separate leaves of rock and their edges through his trousers and pants. He shifted farther down the trench to a place where the leaves were smoothly cut but his backside seemed to fare no better.

"I am who I was."

He examined the shape of his window and the window-box of hair that was flourishing between his two noses. He turned the window down and surveyed all that he could see of himself. The sweater was dragged out into tatters and wisps of wool. It lay in folds beneath his chest and the sleeves were concertina'd. The trousers beneath the sweater were shiny and grey instead of black and beneath them the seaboot stockings drooped like the wads of waste that a stoker wipes his hands on. There was no body to be seen, only a conjunction of worn materials. He eyed the peculiar shapes that lay across the trousers indifferently for a while until at last it occurred to him how strange it was that lobsters should sit there. Then he was suddenly seized with a terrible loathing for lobsters and flung them away so that they cracked on the rock. The dull pain of the blow extended him into them again and they became his hands, lying discarded where he had tossed them.

He cleared his throat as if about to speak in public.

"How can I have a complete identity without a mirror? That is what has changed me. Once I was a man with twenty photographs of myself—myself as this and that with the signature scrawled across the bottom right-hand corner as a stamp and seal. Even when I was in the Navy there was that photograph in my identity card so that every now and then I could look and see who I was. Or perhaps I did not even need to look, but was content to wear the card next to my heart, secure in the knowledge that it was there, proof of me in the round. There were mirrors too, triple mirrors, more separate than the three lights in this window. I could arrange the side ones so that there was a double reflection and spy myself from the side or back in the reflected mirror as though I were watching a stranger. I could spy myself and assess the impact of Christopher Hadley Martin on the world. I could find assurance of my solidity in the bodies of other people by warmth and caresses and triumphant flesh. I could be a character in a body. But now I am this thing in here, a great many aches of bruised flesh, a bundle of rags and those lobsters on the rock. The three lights of my window are not enough to identify me however sufficient they were in the world. But there were other people to describe me to myself—they fell in love with me, they applauded me, they caressed this body, they defined it for me. There were the people I got the better of, people who disliked me, people who quarrelled with me. Here I have nothing to quarrel with. I am in danger of losing definition. I am an album of snapshots, random, a whole show of trailers of old films. The most I know of my face is the scratch of bristles, an itch, a sense of tingling warmth."

He cried out angrily.

"That's no face for a man! Sight is like exploring the night with a flashlight. I ought to be able to see all round my head——"

He climbed down to the water-hole and peered into the pool. But his reflection was inscrutable. He backed out and went down to the Red Lion among the littered shells. He found a pool of salt water on one of the sea rocks. The pool was an inch deep under the sun with one green-weeded limpet and three anemones. There was a tiny fish, less than an inch long, sunning itself on the bottom. He leaned over the pool, looked through the displayed works of the fish and saw blue sky far down. But no matter how he turned his head he could see nothing but a patch of darkness with the wild outline of hair round the edge.

"The best photograph was the one of me as Algernon. The one as Demetrius wasn't bad, either—and as Freddy with a pipe. The make-up took and my eyes looked really wide apart. There was the Night Must Fall one. And that one from The Way of the World. Who was I? It would have been fun playing opposite Jane. That wench was good for a tumble."

The rock hurt the scar on the front of his right thigh. He shifted his leg and peered back into the pool. He turned his head sideways again, trying to catch the right angle for his profile—the good profile, the left one, elevated a little and with a half-smile. But first a shadowy nose and then the semicircle of an eye socket got in the way. He turned back to inquire of his full face but his breathing ruffled the water. He puffed down and the dark head wavered and burst. He jerked up and there was a lobster supporting his weight at the end of his right sleeve.

He made the lobster into a hand again and looked down at the pool. The little fish hung in sunshine with a steady trickle of bubbles rising by it from the oxygen tube. The bottles at the back of the bar loomed through the aquarium as cliffs of jewels and ore.

"No, thanks, old man, I've had enough."

"He's had enough. Ju hear that, George? Ju hear?"

"Hear what, Pete?"

"Dear ol' Chris has had enough."

"Come on, Chris."

"Dear ol' Chris doesn't drink 'n doesn't smoke."

"Likes company, old man."

"Likes company. My company. I'm disgusted with myself. Yur not goin' to say 'Time, Gentlemen, please', miss, are you, gentlemen? He promised his old mother. He said. She said. She said, Chris, my child, let the ten commandments look after themselves she said. But don't drink and don't smoke. Only foke, I beg your pardon, miss, had I known such an intemperate word would have escaped the barrier of my teeth I would have taken steps to have it indictated in the sex with an obelisk or employed a perifris."

"Come on, Pete. Take his other arm, Chris."

"Unhand me, Gentlemen. By heaven I'll make a fish of him that lets me. I am a free and liberal citizen of this company with a wife and child of indifferent sex."

"It's a boy, old man."

"Confidently, George, it's not the sex but the wisdom. Does it know who I am? Who we are? Do you love me, George?"

"You're the best producer we've ever had, you drunken old soak."

"I meant soak, miss. George, you're the most divinely angelic director the bloody theatre ever had and Chris is the best bloody juvenile, aren't you, Chris?"

"Anything you say, eh, George?"

"Definitely, old man, definitely."

"So we all owe everything to the best bloody woman in the world. I love you, Chris. Father and mother is one flesh. And so my uncle. My prophetic uncle. Shall I elect you to my club?"

"How about toddling home, now, Pete?"

"Call it the Dirty Maggot Club. You member? You speak Chinese? You open sideways or only on Sundays?"

"Come on, Pete."

143

"We maggots are there all the week. Y'see when the Chinese want to prepare a very rare dish they bury a fish in a tin box. Presently all the lil' maggots peep out and start to eat. Presently no fish. Only maggots. It's no bloody joke being a maggot. Some of 'em are phototropic. Hey, George—phototropic!"

"What of it, Pete?"

"Phototropic. I said phototropic, miss."

"Finish your maggots, Pete and let's go."

"Oh, the maggots. Yes, the maggots. They haven't finished yet. Only got to the fish. It's a lousy job crawling round the inside of a tin box and Denmark's one of the worst. Well, when they've finished the fish, Chris, they start on each other."

"Cheerful thought, old man."

"The little ones eat the tiny ones. The middle-sized ones eat the little ones. The big ones eat the middle-sized ones. Then the big ones eat each other. Then there are two and then one and where there was a fish there is now one huge, successful maggot. Rare dish."

"Got his hat, George?"

"Come on, Pete! Now careful——"

"I love you, Chris, you lovely big hunk. Eat me."

"Get his arm over your shoulder."

"There's nearly half of me left'n, I'm phototropic. You eat George yet? 'N when there's only one maggot left the Chinese dig it up——"

"You can't sit down here, you silly sot!"

144

"Chinese dig it up——"

"For Christ's sake, stop shouting. We'll have a copper after us."

"Chinese dig it up——"

"Snap out of it, Pete. How the hell do the Chinese know when to dig it up?"

"They know. They got X-ray eyes. Have you ever heard a spade knocking on the side of a tin box, Chris? Boom! Boom! Just like thunder. You a member?"

There was a round of ripples by the three rocks. He watched them intently. Then a brown head appeared by the rocks, another and another. One of the heads had a silver knife across its mouth. The knife bent, flapped and he saw the blade was a fish. The seal heaved itself on to the rock while the others dived, leaving dimpled water and circles. The seal ate, calmly in the sun, rejected the head and tail and lay quiet.

"I wonder if they know about men?"

He stood up slowly and the seal turned its head towards him so that he found himself flinching from an implacable stare. He raised his arms suddenly in the gesture of a man who points a gun. The seal heaved round on the rock and dived. It knew about men.

"If I could get near I could kill it and make boots and eat the meat——"

The men lay on the open beach, wrapped in skins. They endured the long wait and the stench. At dusk, great beasts came out of the sea, played round them, then lay down to sleep.

"An oilskin rolled up would look enough like a seal. When they were used to it I should be inside."

He examined the thought of days. They were a recession like repeated rooms in mirrors hung face to face. All at once he experienced a weariness so intense that it was a pain. He laboured up to the Look-out through the pressure of the sky and all the vast quiet. He made himself examine the empty sea in each quarter. The water was smoother to-day as though the dead air were flattening it. There was shot silk in swathes, oily-looking patches that became iridescent as he watched, like the scum in a ditch. But the wavering of this water was miles long so that a molten sun was elongated, pulled out to nothing here to appear there in a different waver with a sudden blinding dazzle.

"The weather changed while I was in the Red Lion with George and Pete."

He saw a seal head appear for a moment beyond the three rocks and had a sudden wild sight of himself riding a seal across the water to the Hebrides.

"Oh, my God!"

The sound of his voice, flat, yet high and agonized, intimidated him. He dropped his arms and huddled down in his body by the Dwarf. A stream of muttered words began to tumble through the hole under his window.

"It's like those nights when I was a kid, lying awake

thinking the darkness would go on for ever. And I couldn't go back to sleep because of the dream of the whatever it was in the cellar coming out of the corner. I'd lie in the hot, rumpled bed, hot burning hot, trying to shut myself away and know that there were three eternities before the dawn. Everything was the night world, the other world where everything but good could happen, the world of ghosts and robbers and horrors, of things harmless in the daytime coming to life, the wardrobe, the picture in the book, the story, coffins, corpses, vampires, and always squeezing, tormenting darkness, smoke thick. And I'd think of anything because if I didn't go on thinking I'd remember whatever it was in the cellar down there, and my mind would go walking away from my body and go down three stories defenceless, down the dark stairs past the tall, haunted clock, through the whining door, down the terrible steps to where the coffin ends were crushed in the walls of the cellar—and I'd be held helpless on the stone floor, trying to run back, run away, climb up——"

He was standing, crouched. The horizon came back.

"Oh, my God!"

Waiting for the dawn, the first bird cheeping in the eaves or the tree-tops. Waiting for the police by the smashed car. Waiting for the shell after the flash of the gun.

The ponderous sky settled a little more irresistibly on his shoulders.

"What's the matter with me? I'm adult. I know what's what. There's no connection between me and the kid in

147

the cellar, none at all. I grew up. I firmed my life. I have it under control. And anyway there's nothing down there to be frightened of. Waiting for the result. Waiting for that speech—not the next one after this, I know that, but where I go across and take up the cigarette-box. There's a black hole where that speech ought to be and he said you fluffed too much last night, old man. Waiting for the wound to be dressed. This will hurt a little. Waiting for the dentist's chair.

"I don't like to hear my voice falling dead at my mouth like a shot bird."

He put a hand up to either side of his window and watched two black lines diminish it. He could feel the roughness of bristles under either palm and the heat of cheeks.

"What's crushing me?"

He turned his sight round the horizon and the only thing that told him when he had completed the circle was the brighter waver under the sun.

"I shall be rescued any day now. I must not worry. Trailers out of the past are all right but I must be careful when I see things that never happened, like—I have water and food and intelligence and shelter."

He paused for a moment and concentrated on the feeling in the flesh round his window. His hands and skin felt lumpy. He swivelled his eyes sideways and saw that there might indeed be a slight distortion of the semicircle of the eye-hollows.

"Heat lumps? When it rains I shall strip and have a bath. If I haven't been rescued by then."

He pressed with the fingers of his right hand the skin round his eyes. There were heat lumps on the side of his face, that extended down beneath the bristles. The sky pressed on them but they knew no other feeling.

"I must turn in. Go to bed. And stay awake."

The day went grey and hot. Dreary.

"I said I should be sick. I said I must watch out for symptoms."

He went down to the water-hole and crawled in. He drank until he could hear water washing about in his belly. He crawled out backwards and dimensions were mixed up. The surface of the rock was far too hard, far too bright, far too near. He could not gauge size at all.

There was no one else to say a word.

You're not looking too good, old man.

"How the hell can I tell how I look?"

He saw a giant impending and flinched before he could connect the silver head with his chocolate paper. He felt that to stand up would be dangerous for a reason he was not able to formulate. He crawled to the crevice and arranged the clothing. He decided that he must wear everything. Presently he lay with his head out of the crevice on an inflated lifebelt. The sky was bright blue again but very heavy. The opening under his bristles dribbled on.

"Care Charmer Sleep. Cracker mottoes. Old tags. Rag bag of a brain. But don't sleep because of the cellar. How sleep the brave. Nat's asleep. And old gin-soak. Rolled along the bottom or drifting like an old bundle. This is high adventure and anyone can have it. Lie down, rat. Accept your cage. How much rain in this month? How many convoys? How many planes? My hands are larger. All my body is larger and tenderer. Emergency. Action stations. I said I should be ill. I can feel the old scar on my leg tingling more than the rest. Salt in my trousers. Ants in my pants."

He hutched himself sideways in the crevice and withdrew his right hand. He felt his cheek with it but the cheek was dry.

"The tingling can't be sweat, then."

He got his hand back and scratched in his crutch. The edge of the duffle was irritating his face. He remembered that he ought to be wearing the balaclava but was too exhausted to find it. He lay still and his body burned.

He opened his eyes and the sky was violet over him. There was an irregularity in the eye sockets. He lay there, his eyes unfocused and thought of the heat lumps on his face. He wondered if they would close the sockets altogether.

Heat lumps.

The burnings and shiverings of his body succeeded each other as if they were going over him in waves. Suddenly they were waves of molten stuff, solder, melted lead, heated acid, so thick that it moved like oil. Then he was fighting and crying to get out of the crevice.

150

He knelt, shaking on the rock. He put his hands down and they hurt when he leaned his weight on them. He peered down at them first with one eye then the other. They swelled and diminished with a slow pulsing.

"That's not real. Thread of Life. Hang on. That's not real."

But what was real was the mean size of the hands. They were too big even on the average, butcher's hands so full of blood that their flesh was pulpy and swollen. His elbows gave way and he fell between his hands. His cheek was against the uniquely hard rock, his mouth open and he was looking blearily back into the crevice. The waves were still in his body and he recognized them. He gritted his teeth and hung on to himself in the centre of his globe.

"That must mean I'm running a temperature of well over a hundred. I ought to be in hospital."

Smells. Formalin. Ether. Meth. Idioform. Sweet chloroform. Iodine.

Sights. Chromium. White sheets. White bandages. High windows.

Touches. Pain, Pain, Pain.

Sounds. Forces programme drooling like a cretin in the ears from the headphones hitched under the fever chart.

Tastes. Dry lips.

He spoke again with intense solemnity and significance.

"I must go sick."

He lugged the clothes off his body. Before he had got down to his vest and pants the burning was intolerable so that he tore off his clothes and threw them anywhere. He stood up naked and the air was hot on his body, but the action of being naked seemed to do something, for his body started to shiver. He sat painfully on the wall by the white scar of the Claudian and his teeth chattered.

"I must keep going somehow."

But the horizon would not stay still. Like his hands, the sea pulsed. At one moment the purple line was so far away that it had no significance and the next, so close that he could stretch out his arm and lay hold.

"Think. Be intelligent."

He held his head with both hands and shut his eyes.

"Drink plenty of water."

He opened his eyes and the High Street pulsed below him. The rock was striped with lines of seaweed that he saw presently were black shadows cast by the sun and not seaweed at all. The sea beyond the High Street was dead flat and featureless so that he could have stepped down and walked on it, only his feet were swollen and sore. He took his body with great care to the water-hole and pulled himself in. At once he was refrigerated. He put his face in the water and half-gulped, half-ate it with chattering teeth. He crawled away to the crevice.

"The squeezing did it, the awful pressure. It was the weight of the sky and the air. How can one human body support all that weight without bruising into a pulp?"

He made a little water in the trench. The reptiles were floating back to the sea round the rock. They said nothing

152

but sat on the flat sea with their legs hidden.

"I need a crap. I must see about that. Now I must wear everything and sweat this heat out of my body."

By the time he had pulled on all his clothing dusk was come and he felt his way into the crevice with his legs. The crevice enlarged and became populous. There were times when it was larger than the rock, larger than the world, times when it was a tin box so huge that a spade knocking at the side sounded like distant thunder. Then after that there was a time when he was back in rock and distant thunder was sounding like the knocking of a spade against a vast tin box. All the time the opening beneath his window was dribbling on like the Forces Programme, cross-talking and singing to people whom he could not see but knew were there. For a moment or two he was home and his father was like a mountain. The thunder and lightning were playing round the mountain's head and his mother was weeping tears like acid and knitting a sock without a beginning or end. The tears were a kind of charm for after he had felt them scald him they changed the crevice into a pattern.

The opening spoke.

"She is sorry for me on this rock."

Sybil was weeping and Alfred. Helen was crying. A bright boy face was crying. He saw half-forgotten but now clearly remembered faces and they were all weeping.

"That is because they know I am alone on a rock in the middle of a tin box."

They wept tears that turned them to stone faces in a wall, masks hung in rows in a corridor without beginning or end. There were notices that said No Smoking, Gentlemen, Ladies, Exit and there were many uniformed attendants. Down there was the other room, to be avoided, because there the gods sat behind their terrible knees and feet of black stone, but here the stone faces wept and had wept. Their stone cheeks were furrowed, they were blurred and only recognizable by some indefinite mode of identity. Their tears made a pool on the stone floor so that his feet were burned to the ankles. He scrabbled to climb up the wall and the scalding stuff welled up his ankles to his calves, his knees. He was struggling, half-swimming, half-climbing. The wall was turning over, curving like the wall of a tunnel in the underground. The tears were no longer running down the stone to join the burning sea. They were falling freely, dropping on him. One came, a dot, a pearl, a ball, a globe, that moved on him, spread. He began to scream. He was inside the ball of water that was burning him to the bone and past. It consumed him utterly. He was dissolved and spread throughout the tear an extension of sheer, disembodied pain.

He burst the surface and grabbed a stone wall. There was hardly any light but he knew better than to waste time because of what was coming. There were projections in the wall of the tunnel so that though it was more nearly a well than a tunnel he could still climb. He laid hold, pulled himself up, projection after projection. The light was bright enough to show him the projections. They were faces, like the ones in the endless corridor. They were not weeping but they were trodden. They appeared to be made of some chalky material for when he put his weight on them they would break away so that only by constant movement upward was he able to keep up at all. He could hear his voice shouting in the well.

"I am! I am! I am!"

And all the time there was another voice that hung in his ears like the drooling of the Forces Programme. Nobody paid any attention to this voice but the nature of the cretin was to go on talking even though it said the same thing over and over again. This voice had some connection with the lower part of his own face and leaked on as he climbed and broke the chalky, convenient faces.

"Tunnels and wells and drops of water all this is old stuff. You can't tell me. I know my stuff just sexual images from the unconscious, the libido, or is it the id? All explained and known. Just sexual stuff what can you expect? Sensation, all tunnels and wells and drops of water. All old stuff, you can't tell me. I know."

10

A tongue of summer lightning licked right inside the inner crevice so that he saw shapes there. Some were angled and massive as the corners of corridors and between them was the light falling into impenetrable distances. One shape was a woman who unfroze for that instant and lived. The lightning created or discovered her in the act of breathing in; and so nearly was that breath finished that she seemed only to check and breathe out again. He knew without thinking who she was and where she was and when, he knew why she was breathing so quickly, lifting the silk blouse with apples, the forbidden fruit, knew why there were patches of colour on either cheek-bone and why the flush had run as it so uniquely did into the nose. Therefore she presented to him the high forehead, the remote and unconquered face with the three patches of pink arranged across the middle. As for the eyes, they fired an ammunition of contempt and outrage. They were eyes that confirmed all the unworded opinions of his body and fevered head. Seen as a clothed body or listened to, she was common and undistinguished. But the eyes belonged to some other person for they had nothing to do with the irregularity of the face or the aspirations, prudish and social, of the voice. There was the individual, Mary, who was nothing but the intersection of influences from the cradle up, the Mary gloved and hatted for church, she Mary who ate with such maddening refinement, the Mary who carried, poised on her two little feet, a treasure of demoniac and musky attractiveness that was all the more terrible because she was almost unconscious of it. This intersection was so inevitably constructed that its every word and action could be predicted. The intersection would choose the ordinary rather than the exceptional; would fly to what was respectable as to a magnet. It was a fit companion for the pursed-up mouth, the too high forehead, the mousey hair. But the eyes—they had nothing in common with the mask of flesh that nature had fixed on what must surely be a real and invisible face. They were one with the incredible smallness of the waist and the apple breasts, the transparency of the flesh. They were large and wise with a wisdom that never reached the surface to be expressed in speech. They gave to her many silences—so explicable in terms of the intersection—a mystery that was not there. But combined with the furious musk, the little guarded breasts, the surely impregnable virtue, they were the death sentence of Actaeon. They made her occupy as by right, a cleared space in the world behind the eyes that was lit by flickers of summer lightning. They made her a madness, not so much in the loins as in the pride, the need to assert and break, a blight in the growing point of life.

They brought back the nights of childhood, the hot, eternal bed with seamed sheets, the desperation. The things she did became important though they were trivial, the very onyx she wore became a talisman. A thread from her tweed skirt—though she had bought it off the hook in a shop where identical skirts hung empty and unchanged—that same thread was magicked into power by association. Her surname—and he thumped rock with lifted knees—her surname now abandoned to dead Nathaniel forced him to a reference book lest it should wind back to some distinction that would set her even more firmly at the centre than she was. By what chance, or worse what law of the universe was she set there in the road to power and success, unbreakable yet tormenting with the need to conquer and break? How could she take this place behind the eyes as by right when she was nothing but another step on which one must place the advancing foot? Those nights of imagined copulation, when one thought not of love nor sensation nor comfort nor triumph, but of torture rather, the very rhythm of the body reinforced by hissed ejaculations—take that and that! That for your pursed mouth and that for your pink patches, your closed knees, your impregnable balance on the high, female shoes—and that if it kills you for your magic and your isled virtue!

How can she so hold the centre of my darkness when the only real feeling I have for her is hate?

Pale face, pink patches. The last chance and I know what she is going to say, inevitably out of the intersection.

And here it comes quickly, with an accent immediately elevated to the top drawer.

"No."

There are at least three vowels in the one syllable.

"Why did you agree to come here with me, then?"

Three patches.

"I thought you were a gentleman."

Inevitably.

"You make me tired."

"Take me home, please."

"Do you really mean that in the twentieth century? You really feel insulted? You don't just mean 'No, I'm sorry, but no'?"

"I want to go home."

"But look———"

I must, I must, don't you understand you bloody bitch?

"Then I'll take a bus."

One chance. Only one.

"Wait a minute. Our language is so different. Only what I'm trying to say is—well, it's difficult. Only don't you understand that I—Oh Mary, I'll do anything to prove it to you!"

"I'm sorry. I just don't care for you in that way."

And then he, compelled about the rising fury to tread the worn path:

"Then it's still—no?"

Ultimate insult of triumph, understanding and compassion.

"I'm sorry, Chris. Genuinely sorry."

"You'll be a sister to me, I know."

But then the astonishing answer, serenely, brushing away the sarcasm.

"If you like."

He got violently to his feet.

"Come on. Let's get out of here for Christ's sake."

Wait, like a shape in the driving seat. Does she know nothing of me at all? She comes from the road house, one foot swerved in front of the other as in the photographs, walking an invisible tight-rope across the gravel, bearing proudly the invincible banner of virginity.

"That door's not properly shut. Let me."

Subtle the scent, the touch of the cheap, transmuted tweed, hand shaking on the gear, road drawing back, hooded wartime lights, uncontrollable summer lightning ignoring the regulations from beyond that hill to away south in seven-league boots, foot hard down, fringes of leaves jagged like a painted drop, trees touched, brought into being by sidelights and bundled away to the limbo of lost chances.

"Aren't you driving rather fast?"

Tilted cheek, pursed mouth, eyes under the foolish hat, remote, blacked out. Foot hard down.

"Please drive slower, Chris!"

Tyre-scream, gear-whine, thrust and roar——

"Please——!"

Rock, sway, silk hiss of skid, scene film-flicking.

Power.

"Please! Please!"

"Let me, then. Now. Tonight, in the car."

"Please!"

Hat awry, road unravelled, tree-tunnel drunk up——

"I'll kill us."

"You're mad—oh, please!"

"Where the road forks at the whitewashed tree, I'll hit it with your side. You'll be burst and bitched."

"Oh God, oh God."

Over the verge, clout on the heap of dressing, bump, swerve back, eating macadam, drawing it in, pushing it back among the lost chances, pushing it down with time back to the cellar——

"I'm going to faint."

"You'll let me make love to you? Love to you?"

"Please stop."

On the verge, trodden with two feet to a stop, with dead engine and lights, grabbing a stuffed doll, plundering a doll that came to life under the summer lightning, knees clapped together over the hoarded virginity, one hand pushing down the same tweed skirt, one to ward off, finding with her voice a protection for the half-naked breast——

"I shall scream!"

"Scream away."

"You filthy, beastly——"

Then the summer lightning over a white face with two

161

staring eyes only a few inches away, eyes of the artificial woman, confounded in her pretences and evasion, forced to admit her own crude, human body—eyes staring now in deep and implacable hate.

Nothing out of the top drawer now. Vowels with the burr of the country on them.

"Don't you understand, you swine? You can't——"

The last chance. I must.

"I'll marry you then."

More summer lightning.

"Chris. Stop laughing. D'you hear? Stop it! I said stop it!"

"I *loathe* you. I never want to see you or hear of you as long as I live."

Peter was riding behind him and they were flat out. It was his new bike under him but it was not as good as Peter's new one. If Peter got past with that new gear of his he'd be uncatchable. Peter's front wheel was overlapping his back one in a perfect position. He'd never have done that if he weren't deadly excited. The road curves here to the right, here by the pile of dressing. They are built up like rock—a great pile of stones for mending the road down to Hodson's Farm. Don't turn, go straight on, keep going for the fraction of a second longer than he expects. Let him turn, with his overlapping wheel. Oh clever, clever, clever. My leg, Chris, my leg—I daren't look at my leg. Oh Christ.

The cash-box. Japanned tin, gilt lines. Open empty. What are you going to do about it, there was nothing written down. Have a drink with me some time.

She's the producer's wife, old boy.

Oh clever, clever, clever power, then you can bloody well walk home; oh clever, real tears break down triumph, clever, clever, clever.

Up stage. Up stage. Up stage. I'm a bigger maggot than you are. You can't get any further up stage because of the table, but I can go all the way up to the french window.

"No, old man. I'm sorry, but you're not essential."

"But George—we've worked together! You know me——"

"I do, old man. Definitely."

"I should be wasted in the Forces. You've seen my work.

"I have, old man."

"Well then——"

The look up under the eyebrows. The suppressed smile. The smile allowed to spread until the white teeth were reflected in the top of the desk.

"I've been waiting for something like this. That's why I didn't kick you out before. I hope they mar your profile, old man. The good one."

There were ten thousand ways of killing a man. You

could poison him and watch the smile turn into a rictus. You could hold his throat until it was like a hard bar.

She was putting on a coat.

"Helen——"

"My sweet."

The move up, vulpine, passionate.

"It's been so long."

Deep, shuddering breath.

"Don't be corny, dear."

Fright.

"Help me, Helen, I must have your help."

Black maggot eyes in a white face. Distance. Calculation. Death.

"Anything my sweet, but of course."

"After all you're Pete's wife."

"So crude, Chris."

"You could persuade him."

Down close on the settee, near.

"Helen——"

"Why don't you ask Margot, my sweet, or that little thing you took out driving?"

Panic. Black eyes in a white face with no more expression than hard, black stones.

Eaten.

Nathaniel bubbling over in a quiet way—not a bubble over, a simmer, almost a glow.

"I have wonderful news for you, Chris."

"You've met an aeon at last."

Nat considered this, looking up at the reference library. He identified the remark as a joke and answered it with the too profound tones he reserved for humour.

"I have been introduced to one by proxy."

"Tell me your news. Is the war over? I can't wait."

Nathaniel sat down in the opposite armchair but found it too low. He perched himself on the arm, then got up and rearranged the books on the table. He looked into the street between the drab black-out curtains.

"I think finally, I shall go into the Navy."

"You!"

Nodding, still looking out of the window:

"If they'd have me, that is. I couldn't fly and I shouldn't be any use in the Army."

"But you clot! You don't have to go, do you?"

"Not—legally."

"I thought you objected to war."

"So I do."

"Conchie."

"I don't know. I really don't know. One thinks this and that—but in the end, you know, the responsibility of deciding is too much for one man. I ought to go."

"You've made your mind up?"

"Mary agrees with me."

"Mary Lovell? What's she got to do with it?"

"That's my news."

Nathaniel turned with a forgotten book in his hands.

He came towards the fire, looked at the armchair, remembered the book and put it on the table. He took a chair, drew it forward and perched on the edge.

"I was telling you after the show last night. You remember? About how our lives must reach right back to the roots of time, be a trail through history?"

"I said you were probably Cleopatra."

Nat considered this gravely.

"No, I don't think so. Nothing so famous."

"Henry the Eighth, then. Is that your news?"

"One constantly comes across clues. One has—flashes of insight—things given. One is——" The hands began to spread sideways by the shoulders as though they were feeling an expansion of the head—"One is conscious when meeting people that they are woven in with one's secret history. Don't you think? You and I, for example. You remember?"

"You used to talk an awful lot of cock."

Nathaniel nodded.

"I still do. But we are still interwoven and the same things hold good. Then when you introduce me to Mary—you remember? You see how we three act and re-act. There came that sudden flash, that—stab of knowledge and certainty that said, 'I have known you before.'"

"What on earth are you talking about?"

"She felt it too. She said so. She's so—wise, you know! And now we are both quite certain. These things are written in the stars, of course, but under them, Chris, we have to thank you for bringing us together."

"You and Mary Lovell?"

"Of course these things are never simple and we've meditated apart from each other and together——"

An enchantment was filling the room. Nat's head seemed to grow large and small with it.

"And I should be awfully pleased, Chris, if you'd be best man for me."

"You're going to marry! You and——"

"That was the joyous news."

"You can't!"

He heard how anguished his voice was, found he was standing up.

Nat looked past him into the fire.

"I know it's sudden but we've meditated. And you see, I shall be going into the Navy. She's so good and brave. And you, Chris—I knew you would bring your whole being to such a decision."

He stood still, looking down at the tousled black hair, the length of limb. He felt the bleak recognition rising in him of the ineffable strength of these circumstances and this decision. Not where he eats but where he is eaten. Blood rose with the recognition, burning in the face, power to break. Pictures of her fell through his mind like a dropped sheaf of snapshots—Mary in the boat, carefully arranging her skirt; Mary walking to church, reeking of it, the very placing of her feet and carriage of her little bum an insolence; Mary struggling, knees clapped

167

together over the hoarded virginity, trying with one hand to pull down her skirt, with the other to ward off, the voice finding the only protection for her half-naked breast——

"I shall scream!"

Nat looked up, his mouth open.

"I'm not being a fool this time you know. You needn't worry."

The snapshots vanished.

"I was—I don't know what I was saying, Nat—quoting from some play or other."

Nat spread his hands and smiled diffidently.

"The stars can't be thwarted."

"Especially if they happen to agree with what you want."

Nat considered this. He reddened a little and nodded gravely.

"There is that danger."

"Be careful, Nat, for God's sake."

But not known, not understood—what is he to be careful of? Of staying near me? Of standing with her in the lighted centre of my darkness?

"You'll be here to look after her, Chris, when I've gone."

There is something in the stars. Or what is this obscure impulse that sets my words at variance with my heart?

"Only be careful. Of me."

"Chris!"

Because I like you, you fool and hate you. And now I hate you.

168

"All right, Nat, forget it."

"There's something the matter."

An impulse gone, trodden down, kicked aside.

"I shall be in the Navy, too."

"But the theatre!"

Gone down under calculation and hate.

"One has one's better feelings."

"My dear man!" Nat was standing and beaming. "Perhaps we can be in the same ship."

Drearily and with the foreknowledge of a chosen road.

"I'm sure we shall be. That's in our stars."

Nat nodded.

"We are connected in the elements. We are men for water."

"Water. Water."

The clothes bound him like a soggy bundle. He hauled himself out into the sun. He lay there feeling that he spread like seaweed. He got his hands up and plucked at the toggles of his duffle while the snapshots whirled and flew like a pack of cards. He got the toggles free and plucked at the rest of his clothing. When he had only vest and pants on he crawled away, yards over the rock to the water-hole. He crawled up the High Street and lay down by the Dwarf.

"If I am not delirious this is steam rising from my clothes. Sweat."

He propped his back against the Dwarf.

"Be intelligent."

His legs before him were covered with white blotches. There were more on his stomach when he lifted his vest, on his arms and legs. They were deformations at the edge of the eye-sockets.

"Stay alive!"

Something fierce pushed out of his mind.

"I'll live if I have to eat everything else on this bloody box!"

He looked down at his legs.

"I know the name for you bloody blotches. Urticaria. Food poisoning."

He lay quiet for a time. The steam rose and wavered. The blotches were well-defined and of a dead whiteness. They were raised so that even swollen fingers could feel their outline.

"I said I should be ill and I am."

He peered hazily round the horizon but it had nothing to give. He looked back at his legs and decided that they were very thin for all the blotches. Under his vest he could feel the trickle of water that found its way down from blotch to blotch.

The pressure of the sky and air was right inside his head.

11

A thought was forming like a piece of sculpture behind the eyes but in front of the unexamined centre. He watched the thought for a timeless interim while the drops of sweat trickled down from blotch to blotch. But he knew that the thought was an enemy and so although he saw it he did not consent or allow it to become attached to him in realization. If the slow centre had any activity now it brooded on its identity while the thought stayed there like an ignored monument in a park. Christopher and Hadley and Martin were separate fragments and the centre was smouldering with a dull resentment that they should have broken away and not be sealed on the centre. The window was filled with a pattern of colour but in this curious state the centre did not think of the pattern as exterior. It was the only visible thing in a dark room, like a lighted picture on the wall. Below it was the sensation of water trickling and discomfort of a hard surface. The centre for a time was sufficient. The centre knew self existed, though Christopher and Hadley and Martin were fragments far off.

A curtain of hair and flesh fell over the picture on

the wall and there was nothing to be examined but the thought. It became known. The terror that swept in with the thought shocked him into the use of his body. There was a flashing of nerves, tensing of muscles, heaves, blows, vibration; and the thought became words that tumbled out of his mouth.

"I shall never get away from this rock."

The terror did more. It straightened the hinged bones and stood him up, sent him reeling round the Look-out in the pressure of the sky till he was clinging to the Dwarf and the stone head was rocking gently, rocking gently, and the sun was swinging to and fro, up and down in the silver face.

"Get me off this rock!"

The Dwarf nodded its silver head, gently, kindly.

He crouched down by a whitish trench and the pattern of colour was sight again.

Christopher and Hadley and Martin came part way back. He forced the pattern to fit everywhere over the rock and the sea and the sky.

"Know your enemy."

There was illness of the body, effect of exposure. There was food-poisoning that made the world a mad place. There was solitude and hope deferred. There was the thought; there were the other thoughts, unspoken and un-admitted.

"Get them out. Look at them."

Water, the only supply, hung by a hair, held back by the slimy tamping; food that grew daily less; pressure, indescribable pressure on the body and the mind; battle with the film-trailers for sleep. There was——

"There was and is——"

He crouched on the rock.

"Take it out and look at it.

"There is a pattern emerging. I do not know what the pattern is but even my dim guess at it makes my reason falter."

The lower half of his face moved round the mouth till the teeth were bare.

"Weapons. I have things that I can use."

Intelligence. Will like a last ditch. Will like a monolith. Survival. Education, a key to all patterns, itself able to impose them, to create. Consciousness in a world asleep. The dark, invulnerable centre that was certain of its own sufficiency.

He began to speak against the flat air, the blotting-paper.

"Sanity is the ability to appreciate reality. What is the reality of my position? I am alone on a rock in the middle of the Atlantic. There are vast distances of swinging water round me. But the rock is solid. It goes down and joins the floor of the sea and that is joined to the floors I have known, to the coasts and cities. I must remember that the rock is solid and immovable. If the rock were to move then I should be mad."

A flying lizard flapped overhead, and dropped down out of sight.

"I must hang on. First to my life and then to my sanity. I must take steps."

He dropped the curtains over the window again.

"I am poisoned. I am in servitude to a coiled tube the length of a cricket pitch. All the terrors of hell can come down to nothing more than a stoppage. Why drag in good and evil when the serpent lies coiled in my own body?"

And he pictured his bowels deliberately, the slow, choked peristaltic movement, change of the soft food to a plug of poison.

"I am Atlas. I am Prometheus."

He felt himself loom, gigantic on the rock. His jaws clenched, his chin sank. He became a hero for whom the impossible was an achievement. He knelt and crawled remorselessly down the rock. He found the lifebelt in the crevice, took his knife and sawed the metal tit away from the tube. He crawled on down towards the Red Lion and now there was background music, snatches of Tchaikovsky, Wagner, Holst. It was not really necessary to crawl but the background music underlined the heroism of a slow, undefeated advance against odds. The empty mussel shells cracked under his bones like potsherds. The music swelled and was torn apart by brass.

He came to the pool on the rock with the one weedy limpet and three prudish anemones. The tiny fish still lay in the water but on a different part of the rock. He pushed the lifebelt under the surface of the water so that the fish flicked desperately from side to side. A string of bubbles

174

came out of the tube. He collapsed the long bladder and then began to pull it open again. Little spits of water entered the tit and worked down between more bubbles. Strings only, now, deep. He lifted the whole lifebelt out and hefted the bag. There was a washing sound from the bladder. He sank it in the pool again and went on working. The strings were working too, and woodwind was added and a note or two of brass. Presently, and soon there would come the suspended chord that would stand the whole orchestra aside for the cadenza. The weedy top of the limpet was above the surface. The tiny fish, tricked by this unnatural ebb was lying on wet rock in the sun and trying to wriggle against the surface tension. The anemones had shut their mouths even tighter. The bladder of the lifebelt was two-thirds full.

He hutched himself back against a rock with his legs sprawled apart. The music rose, the sea played and the sun. The universe held its breath. Grunting and groaning he began to work the rubber tube into his backside. He folded the two halves of the long bladder together and sat on it. He began to work at the bladder with both hands, squeezing and massaging. He felt the cold trickle of the sea water in his bowels. He pumped and squeezed until the bladder was squashily flat. He extracted the tube and crept carefully to the edge of the rock while the orchestra thundered to a pause.

And the cadenza was coming—did come. It performed with explosive and triumphant completeness of technique into the sea. It was like the bursting of a dam, the smashing of all hindrance. Spasm after spasm with massive chords and sparkling arpeggios, the cadenza took of his strength till he lay straining and empty on the rock and the orchestra had gone.

He turned his face on the rock and grunted at the antagonist.

"Are you beaten yet? I'm not."

The hand of the sky fell on him. He got up and knelt among the mussel shells.

"Now I shall be sane and no longer such a slave to my body."

He looked down at the dead fish. He pushed the body with his finger to the mouth of an anemone. Petals emerged and tried to take hold.

"Stings. Poison. Anemones poisoned me. Perhaps mussels are all right after all."

He felt a little stronger and no longer so heroic that he need crawl. He went slowly back to the Look-out.

"Everything is predictable. I knew I shouldn't drown and I didn't. There was a rock. I knew I could live on it and I have. I have defeated the serpent in my body. I knew I should suffer and I have. But I am winning. There is a certain sense in which life begins anew now, for all the blotting-paper and the pressure."

He sat down by the Dwarf and drew up his knees. His sight was right on the outside and he lived in the world.

"I believe I'm hungry."

176

And why not, when life begins again?

"Food on a plate. Rich food in comfort. Food in shops, butchers' shops, food, not swimming, shutting like a fist and vanishing into a crevice but dead on a slab, heaped up, all the sea's harvest——"

He examined the sea. The tide was running and glossy streaks were tailing away from the three rocks.

"Optical illusion."

For of course the rock was fixed. If it seemed to move slowly forward in the tide that was because the eye had nothing else as a point of reference. But over the horizon was a coast and that remained at a constant distance while the water flowed. He smiled grimly.

"That wasn't a bad trick. It might have caught most people."

Like the train that seems to move backwards when the other one steams away from beside it. Like hatched lines with one across.

"For of course the rock is still and the water moves. Let me work it out. The tide is a great wave that sweeps round the world—or rather the world turns inside the tide, so I and the rock are——"

Hastily he looked down at the rock between his feet.

"So the rock is still."

Food. Heaped on a slab, not swimming free but piled up, all the spoils of the sea, a lobster, not shutting like a fist and shooting back into a crevice but——

He was on his feet. He was glaring down at the place

177

where the weed grew under water by the three rocks. He cried out.

"Whoever saw a lobster like that swimming in the sea? A red lobster?"

Something was taken away. For an instant he felt himself falling; and then there came a gap of darkness in which there was no one.

Something was coming up to the surface. It was uncertain of its identity because it had forgotten its name. It was disorganized in pieces. It struggled to get these pieces together because then it would know what it was. There was a rhythmical noise and disconnection. The pieces came shakily together and he was lying sideways on the rock and a snoring noise was coming from his mouth. There was a feeling of deep sickness further down the tunnel. There was a separation between now, whenever now was, and the instant of terror. The separation enabled him to forget what had caused that terror. The darkness of separation was deeper than that of sleep. It was deeper than any living darkness because time had stopped or come to an end. It was a gap of not-being, a well opening out of the world and now the effort of mere being was so exhausting that he could only lie sideways and live.

Presently he thought.

"Then I was dead. That was death. I have been frightened to death. Now the pieces of me have come together and I am just alive."

178

The view was different too. The three rocks were nearer and there were sharp things—mussel shells, he thought, brilliantly—cutting his cheek.

"Who carried me down here?"

There came a little pain with the words which he traced to his tongue. The tip was swollen, and aching, and there was salt in his mouth. He could see a pair of empty trousers lying near him and curious marks on the rock. These marks were white and parallel. There was blood in them and traces of froth.

He attended to the rest of his body. He identified a hard, bar-like object as his right arm, twisted back. That led him to the pain in the joints. He eased over so that his arm was free and gazed at the hand on the end.

Now he saw that he was not wearing his pants because they were out there in his right hand. They were torn and there was blood on them.

"I've been in a fight."

He lay, considering things dully.

"There is someone else on the rock with me. He crept out and slugged me."

The face twisted.

"Don't be a fool. You're all alone. You've had a fit."

He felt for his left hand and found it with a grunt of pain. The fingers were bitten.

"How long was I? Is it today or yesterday?"

He heaved himself up on hands and knees.

"Just when I was myself again and victorious, there

came a sort of something. A Terror. There was a pattern emerging from circumstances."

Then the gap of not-being.

"This side of the gap is different from the other. It's like when you've finished a lights rehearsal and they cut. Then where there was bright, solid scenery is now only painted stuff, grey under the pilot light. It's like chess. You've got an exultant attack moving but overlooked a check and now the game is a fight. And you're tied down."

Bright rock and sea, hope, though deferred, heroics. Then in the moment of achievement, the knowledge, the terror like a hand falling.

"It was something I remembered. I'd better not remember it again. Remember to forget. Madness?"

Worse than madness. Sanity.

He heaved himself on his hands and knees and laboured to trace his fit, by the scattered clothing and the marks on the rock, back to where he had begun. He stopped by the Dwarf, looking down at rock with a pattern scratched on it—a pattern now crossed by the gritted mark of teeth.

"That was to be expected. Everything is to be expected. The world runs true to form. Remember that."

He looked thoughtfully down at the streaks that the rock was leaving behind in the sea.

"I must not look at the sea. Or must I? Is it better to be sane or mad? It is better to be sane. I did not see what I thought I saw. I remembered wrongly."

Then he had an important idea. It set him at once

180

searching the rock, not in a casual way but inch by inch. Only after an eternity of searching, of cracks and bumps and roughnesses did he remember that he was foolish to search for a piece of wood to touch because there was none.

His pants were still trailing from his hand and he had a sudden thought that he could put them on. When he had done this his head cleared of all the mists except the pain. He put his hand up to the pain and found that there was a lump under the hair and the hair was stuck with blood. He examined his legs. The white blotches were smaller and no longer important. He remembered a custom and clambered into the water-hole. When he was in there he noticed a sudden, bright light in the opening over the far end and some deep seat of rationality drove him back to the Look-out; and he knew what the light and the noise that had come after it portended.

The sun was still shining but there was a change over a part of the horizon. He knelt to look at this change and it was divided again by a vertical jab of light. This light left a token in each eye that made seeing a divided business. He peered round the green streak that the light left and saw that the darkness made a definite line on the surface of the sea. It was coming nearer. Instantly he was in his body and knew where he was.

"Rain!"

Of course.

"I said there would be rain!"

Let there be rain and there was rain.

He scrambled down the High Street, got his sou'wester and arranged it in the lay-back under the end of the Claudian. He pulled off what clothes he was wearing and thrust them into the crevice. He was aware of bright lights and noise. He put his oilskin in a trench and ducked the body into a basin. He went almost upright to the Look-out and heard the hiss of the rain as the edge of the curtain fell on the Safety Rock. It hit him in the face sprang in foot-high leaps from the Dwarf and the surface of the look-out. He glistened and streamed from head to foot in a second.

There was a merciless flash-bang from the curtain and then he was stumbling down to the crevice and burrowing in head first while the thunder trampled overhead. Even in the depth of the crevice he saw a livid light that hurt his ears; and then there was the cessation of all noises but a high, singing note. This was so intimate to the head that it took the place of the thunder. His feet were being bastinadoed. His mouth said things but he could not hear them so did not know what they were. There was water running in the crevice, under his face, dripping from the rock, water running round his loins, water. He made his body back out of the crevice and was under a waterfall. He stumbled into a trench and found his sou'wester full and spilling. There was a tap of water running from the end of the Claudian and he took up the heavy sou'wester and poured water into his mouth. He put the sou'wester

182

back and went to his oilskin. There was a bath ready for him but the rain was washing over him like a shower. He went back to the sou'wester, watched it fill and took it to the water-hole. He could hear the running click and trickle under the rock now—water running down, seaping through in unguessed crannies, falling with a multitudinous chattering into the hollow. Already the stretch of red clay was narrower.

"I said it would rain, and it has."

He waited, shivering in the chilly cave, waited for the satisfaction that ought to come with the fulfilled prediction. But it would not come.

He crouched there, no longer listening to the water but frowning down at his shadow.

"What piece have I lost in my game? I had an attack, I was doing well, and then——" And then, the gap of dark, dividing that brighter time from this. On the other side of the gap was something that had happened. It was something that must not be remembered; but how could you control if you deliberately forgot? It was something about a pattern that was emerging.

"Inimical."

He considered the word that his mouth had spoken. The word sounded harmless unless the implications were attached. To avoid that, he deliberately bent the process of thought and made his mouth do as he bid.

"How can a rock be inimical?"

He crawled away quickly into a rain that fell more

lightly. The storm had hurried away over the three rocks and dulled the motion of the water. The clouds had dulled everything. They had left a grey, drizzly sea over which the air moved, pushed at the rock in a perceptible wind.

"That was a subsidiary thunder-storm on the edge of a cyclone. Cyclones revolve anti-clockwise in the northern hemisphere. The wind is southerly. Therefore we are on the eastern edge of a cyclone that is moving east. Since I can foretell the weather I can be armed against it. The problem will be now to cope with too much water, not too little."

He paid only half-attention to his mouth. It lectured on reassuring nothing but itself. But the centre of the globe was moving and flinching from isolated outcrops of knowledge. It averted attention from one only to discover another. It attempted to obliterate each separate outcrop when it found that they could not be ignored.

"The whole problem of insanity is so complex that a satisfactory definition, a norm, has never been estab-lished."

Far out from the centre, the mouth quacked on.

"Where, for example, shall we draw the line between the man whom we consider to be moody or excitable, and the genuine psychopathic manic-depressive?"

The centre was thinking, with an eye lifted for the re-turn of the storm of terror, about how difficult it was to distinguish between sleeping and waking when all one ex-perienced was a series of trailers.

184

"A recurrent dream, a neurosis? But surely the normal child in its cot goes through all the symptoms of the neurotic?"

If one went step by step—ignoring the gap of dark and the terror on the lip—back from the rock, through the Navy, the stage, the writing, the university, the school, back to bed under the silent eaves, one went down to the cellar. And the path led back from the cellar to the rock.

"The solution lies in intelligence. That is what distinguishes us from the helpless animals that are caught in their patterns of behaviour, both mental and physical."

But the dark centre was examining a thought like a monument that had replaced the other in the dreary park.

Guano is insoluble.

If guano is insoluble, then the water in the upper trench could not be a slimy wetness, the touch of which made a flaming needle nag at the corner of an eye.

His tongue felt along the barrier of his teeth—round to the side where the big ones were and the gap. He brought his hands together and held his breath. He stared at the sea and saw nothing. His tongue was remembering. It pried into the gap between the teeth and re-created the old, aching shape. It touched the rough edge of the cliff, traced the slope down, trench after aching trench, down towards the smooth surface where the Red Lion was, just above the gum—understood what was so hauntingly familiar and painful about an isolated and decaying rock in the middle of the sea.

12

Now there was nothing to do but protect normality. There was the centre wielding the exterior body as by strings. He made the body go down from the Look-out to the crevice. He found damp clothes and put them on until he could see extensions of clothing and seaboot stockings like piles of waste. The body and the clothing were ungainly as a diving dress. He went to Food Cliff and gathered mussels, made his mouth receive them. He did not look outwards but down where the water danced alongside the rock. The sea was ruffled and there were wavelets each carrying smaller wavelets on its back so that the depth was obscured and the water grave and chilly. As his jaws worked he sat still with two lobsters lying on the rock beside him. The meal went on under pricking rain, a stirring of wind and scuds of dimples across the surface of the water. He took morsels of food with one lobster and brought them to his face. The lobsters wore armour to protect them from the enormous pressure of the sky.

Between mouthfuls his voice quacked, veering in to-wards reason and truth and then skating away.

"I have no armour and that is why I am being squeezed thin. It has marred my profile too. My mouth sticks out such a long way and I have two noses."

But the centre thought of other things.

"I must be careful when I look round at the wind. I don't want to die again."

Meanwhile there were many mussels and one could make the mouth perform and obliterate the other possibilities.

"I was always two things, mind and body. Nothing has altered. Only I did not realize it before so clearly."

The centre thought of the next move. The world could be held together by rivets driven in. Flesh could be mended by the claws of ants as in Africa. The will could resist.

And then there were no more mussels within reach. He made the lobster mime eating but the sensations in the mouth were not the same.

"Have to do it."

He turned himself on all fours. He held his breath and looked up and there was the old woman from the corner of the cellar standing on the skyline.

"She is the Dwarf. I gave her a silver head."

Wind pushed in his face and a touch of rain. The old woman nodded with her face of dulled silver.

"It is lucky I put a silver mask over the other face. She is the Dwarf. That is not the next move."

He worked his way back towards the Look-out, carried his body near the Dwarf and made it kneel down. Above him the Dwarf nodded gently with a face of dulled silver.

There was something in the topmost trench that was different. Immediately he flinched back and looked warily. The white stuff in the bottom was broken up and scattered because a chunk of rockleaf had fallen from the side of the trench. He crept forward and examined the chunk. On one edge the leaves were worn and ancient but on the other three they were white as muck and freshly broken. The chunk was about a yard each way and six inches thick. It was a considerable book and there was a strange engraving in the white cover. For a while his eye liked the engraving because it made a pattern and was not words, which would have killed him immediately. His eye followed the indented and gouged lines again and again as his mouth had eaten mussels. By the edge of the book was the recess from which it had come.

There was an engraving in the recess too. It was like a tree upside down and growing down from the old edge where the leaves were weathered by wind and rain. The trunk was a deep, perpendicular groove with flaky edges. Lower down, the trunk divided into three branches and these again into a complication of twigs like the ramifications of bookworm. The trunk and the branches and the twigs were terrible black. Round the twigs was an apple blossom of grey and silver stain. As he watched, drops of water dulled the stain and lay in the branches like tasteless fruit.

His mouth quacked.

"Lightning!"

But the dark centre was shrunk and dreadful and knowing. The knowing was so dreadful that the centre made the mouth work deliberately.

"Black lightning."

There was still a part that could be played—there was the Bedlamite, Poor Tom, protected from knowledge of the sign of the black lightning.

He grabbed the old woman with her nodding silver head.

"Help me, my sweet, I must have your help!"

The mouth took over.

"If you let him go on doing that, my sweet, he'll knock the whole bloody rock apart and we shall be left swimming."

Swimming in what?

The mouth went frantic.

"There was that rock round by Prospect Cliff, my sweet, that one moved, the water moved it. I wouldn't ask anyone but you because the rock is fixed and if he'll only let it alone it'll last for ever. After all, my sweet, you're his wife."

Out of bed on the carpet with no shoes. Creep through the dark room not because you want to but because you've got to. Pass the door. The landing, huge, the grandfather clock. No safety behind me. Round the corner now to the stairs. Down, pad. Down, pad. The hall, but grown. Darkness sitting in every corner. The banisters high up, can just reach them with my hand. Not for sliding down now. Different banisters, everything different, a pattern emerging, forced to go down to meet the thing I turned my back on. Tick, tock, shadows pressing. Past the kitchen door. Draw back the bolt of the vault. Well of darkness. Down pad, down. Coffin ends crushed in the wall. Under the churchyard back through the death door to meet the master. Down, pad, down. Black lumps piled, smell damp. Shavings from coffins.

"A man must be mad when he sees a red lobster swimming in the sea. And guano is insoluble. A madman would see the gulls as flying lizards, he would connect the two things out of a book and it would come back to him when his brain turned no matter how long ago and forgotten the time when he read that—wouldn't he, my sweet? Say he would! Say he would!"

The silver face nodded on gently and the rain spattered.

Kindling from coffins, coal dust, black as black lightning. Block with the axe by it, not worn for firewood but by executions.

"Seals aren't inimical and a madman wouldn't sleep properly. He would feel the rock was too hard, too real; he would superimpose a reality, especially if he had too much imagination. He would be capable of seeing the engraving as a split into the whole nature of things—wouldn't he?"

And then fettered in the darkness by the feet, trying to lift one and finding a glue, finding a weakness where there should be strength now needed because by nature there

190

was nothing to do but scream and try to escape. Darkness in the corner doubly dark, thing looming, feet tied, near, an unknown looming, an opening darkness, the heart and being of all imaginable terror. Pattern repeated from the beginning of time, approach of the unknown thing, a dark centre that turned its back on the thing that created it and struggled to escape.

"Wouldn't he? Say he would!"

There was a noise by his left arm and water scattered across the Look-out. He made the exterior face turn into the wind and the air pushed against the cheeks. The water on the Dwarf now was not rain but spray. He crept to the edge of the cliff and looked down the funnel. The water was white round Safety Rock and as he looked a dull sound in the funnel was followed by a plume of spray.

"This weather has been investigated before but from a lower level. He climbed there and the limpets held on."

There was a gathering rhythm in the sea. The Safety Rock tripped the waves and shot them at the cleft below the funnel. Nine times out of ten these waves would meet a reflection coming back and spurt up a line of spray like a fuse burning—a fast fuse that whipped over the water. But the tenth time the wave would find the way clear because the ninth wave had been a very small one. So the tenth wave would come wheeling in, the cleft would squeeze the water so that it speeded up and hit the back of the angle—bung! and a feather of spray would flicker in the funnel. If the tenth wave was big the feather would become a plume and the wind would catch a handful from the top and sling shot across the Dwarf to go scattering down the High Street.

To watch the waves was like eating mussels. The sea was a point of an attention that could be prolonged even more than eating. The centre concentrated and left the mouth to itself.

"Of course a storm has to come after a time. That was to be expected. And who could invent all that complication of water, running true to form, obeying the laws of nature to the last drop? And of course a human brain must turn in time and the universe be muddled. But beyond the muddle there will still be actuality and a poor mad creature clinging to a rock in the middle of the sea."

There is no centre of sanity in madness. Nothing like this "I" sitting in here, staving off the time that must come. The last repeat of the pattern. Then the black lightning.

The centre cried out.

"I'm so alone! Christ! I'm so alone!"

Black. A familiar feeling, a heaviness round the heart, a reservoir which any moment might flood the eyes now and for so long, strangers to weeping. Black, like the winter evening through which the centre made its body walk—a young body. The window was diversified only by a perspective of lighted lamps on the top of the street lamp-posts. The centre was thinking—I am alone; so alone! The reservoir overflowed, the lights all the way

192

along to Carfax under Big Tom broke up, put out rainbow wings. The centre felt the gulping of its throat, sent eyesight on ahead to cling desperately to the next light and then the next—anything to fasten the attention away from the interior blackness.

Because of what I did I am an outsider and alone.

The centre endured a progress through an alley, across another road, a quadrangle, climbed bare wooden stairs. It sat by a fire and all the bells of Oxford tolled for the reservoir that overflowed and the sea roared in the room.

The centre twisted the unmanliness out of its face but the ungovernable water ran and dripped down the cheeks.

"I am so alone. I am *so* alone!"

Slowly, the water dried. Time stretched out, like the passage of time on a rock in the middle of the sea.

The centre formulated a thought.

Now there is no hope. There is nothing. If they would only look at me, or speak—if I could only be a part of something——

Time stretched on, indifferently.

There was the sound of feet on the stairs, two stories down. The centre waited without hope, to hear which room they would visit. But they came on, they climbed, were louder, almost as loud as the heart-beats so that when they stopped outside the door he was standing up and his hands were by his chest. The door opened a few inches and a shock of black curls poked round by the very top.

"Nathaniel!"

Nathaniel bowed and beamed his way into the room and stood looking down at the window.

"I thought I might catch you. I'm back for the week-end." Then as an afterthought: "Can I come in?"

"My dear man!"

Nathaniel operated on his great-coat, peered round solemnly as though the question of where to put it was a major one.

"Here. Let me take that for you—sit down—I'm—my dear man!"

Nathaniel was grinning too.

"It's good to see you, Christopher."

"And you can stay? You don't have to rush away?"

"I've come up to give a lecture to the——"

"But not this evening?"

"No. I can stay this evening."

The centre sat opposite, right on the outside of its window—right out in the world.

"We'll talk. Let's talk, Nat."

"How's the social whirl?"

"How's London?"

"Doesn't like lectures on heaven."

"Heaven?"

Then the body was laughing, louder and louder and the water was flowing again. Nat was grinning and blushing too.

"I know. But you don't have to make it worse."

He smeared away the water and hiccupped.

"Why heaven?"

"The sort of heaven we invented for ourselves after death, if we aren't ready for the real one."

"You would—you curious creature!"

Nathaniel became serious. He peered upwards, raised an index finger and consulted a reference book beyond the ceiling.

"Take us as we are now and heaven would be sheer negation. Without form and void. You see? A sort of black lightning, destroying everything that we call life——"

The laughter came back.

"I don't see and I don't much care but I'll come to your lecture. My dear Nat—you've no idea how glad I am to see you!"

The burning fuse whipped through Nathaniel's face and he was gone. The centre remained looking down into the funnel. His mouth was open in astonishment and terror.

"And I liked him as much as that!"

Black and feeling one's way to the smooth steel ladder that glinted only faintly in the cloud light. The centre tried to resist, like a child trying to resist a descent into the midnight cellar but its legs bore it on. Up and up, from the waist to the level of the fo'c'sle, up past B gun. Shall I meet him? Will he stand there tonight?

And there, sketched against the clouds in Indian ink, random in limb and gesture, an old binder by a rick, was Nathaniel, swaying and grabbing at a midnight salute. Wotcher, Nat, rose in his throat and he swallowed it. Pretend not to see. Be as little connected as possible. Fire a fuse from the bridge that will blow him away from her body and clear the way for me. We are all past the first course, we have eaten the fish.

And it may not work. He may not bother to lay aft and pray to his aeons. Good-bye, Nat, I loved you and it is not in my nature to love much. But what can the last maggot but one do? Lose his identity?

Nathaniel stood swaying and spread-eagled in the dark, understanding obediently that he had not been seen. Instead he stood away from the officer's approach and fumbled on down the ladder.

Everything set, the time, the place, the loved one.

"You're early for once, thank God. Course o-four-five, speed twenty-eight knots. Nothing in sight and we press on for another hour."

"Anything new?"

"Same as was. We're thirty miles north of the convoy, all on our own, going to send off the signal in an hour's time. The old man'll be up for that. There you are. No zigzag. Dead easy. Oh—the moon'll be up in ten minutes' time and we'd make quite a target if we tripped over a U-boat. Pass it on. Nighty night."

"Sweet dreams."

He heard the steps descending. He crossed to the starboard side of the bridge and looked aft. There was engine-noise, outline of the funnel. The wake spread out dull white astern and a secondary wave fanned out from midships. The starboard side of the quarter-deck was just visible in outline but the surface was dark by contrast and all the complications of the throwers, the depth-charges, the sweeps and lifted gun made it very difficult to see whether there was a figure leaning on the rail among them. He stared down and wondered whether he saw or created in his mind, the mantis shape with forelegs lifted to the face.

It is not Nathaniel leaning there, it is Mary.

I must. I must. Don't you understand, you bloody bitch?

"Messenger!"

"Sir."

"Get me a cup of cocoa."

"Aye aye, sir!"

"And messenger—never mind."

Feet descending the ladder. Darkness and the wind of speed. Glow over to starboard like a distant fire from a raided city. Moonrise.

"Port look-out!"

"Sir?"

"Nip down to the wheel-house and get me the other pair of night-glasses. I think these need overhauling. You'll find them in the rack over the chart table."

"Aye aye, sir!"

"I'll take over your sector while you're gone."

"Aye aye, sir!"

Feet descending the ladder.

Now.

Ham it a bit. Casual saunter to the port side. Pause.

Now. Now. Now.

Scramble to the binnacle, fling yourself at the voice pipe, voice urgent, high, sharp, frightened——

"Hard a-starboard for Christ's sake!"

A destroying concussion that had no part in the play. Whiteness rising like a cloud, universe spinning. The shock of a fall somewhere, shattering, mouth filled—and he was fighting in all directions with black impervious water.

His mouth screamed in rage at the whiteness that rose out of the funnel.

"And it was the right bloody order!"

Eaten.

He was no longer able to look at the waves, for every few minutes they were hidden by the rising whiteness. He made his sight creep out and look at his clothed body. The clothes were wringing wet and the seaboot stockings smeared like mops. His mouth said something mechanical.

"I wish I hadn't kicked off my seaboots when I was in the water."

The centre told itself to pretend and keep on pretend-
ing.

The mouth had its own wisdom.

"There is always madness, a refuge like a crevice in the
rock. A man who has no more defence can always creep into madness like one of those armoured things that scuttle
among weed down where the mussels are."

Find something to look at.

"Madness would account for everything, wouldn't it,
my sweet?"

Do, if not look.

He got up and staggered in the wind with the rain and
spray pelting him. He went down the High Street and
there was his oilskin made into a basin and full of water.
He took his sou'wester and began to bail out the oilskin
and take the water to the water-hole. He concentrated on
the laws of water, how it fell or lay, how predictable it was
and manageable. Every now and then the rock shook, a
white cloud rose past the Look-out and there were rivu-
lets of foam in the upper trenches. When he had emptied
his oilskin he held it up, drained it and put it on. Fooling with buttons the centre could turn away from what
was to come. While he did this he was facing the Claudian
where the foam now hung in gobs and the oilskin thrust
him against the cut. As he stood pinned, he was struck a
blow in the back and bucketfuls of water fell in the trench.
It washed round then settled scummily in the bottom. He
felt his way along the Claudian to the crevice and backed

himself in. He put on his sou'wester and laid his forehead on his arms. The world turned black and came to him through sound.

"If a madman heard it he would think it was thunder and of course it would be. There is no need to listen like that. It will only be thunder over the horizon where the ships are passing to and fro. Listen to the storm instead. It is going to flail on this rock. It is going to beat a poor wretch into madness. He does not want to go mad only he will have to. Think of it! All you people in warm beds, a British sailor isolated on a rock and going mad not because he wants to but because the sea is a terror—the worst terror there is, the worst imaginable."

The centre co-operated but with an ear cocked. It concentrated now on the words that spilt out of the mouth because with the fringes of flesh and hair lowered over the window the words could be examined as the thoughts had been. It provided background music.

"Oh help, help! I am dying of exposure. I am starving, dying of thirst. I lie like driftwood caught in a cleft. I have done my duty for you and this is my reward. If you could only see me you would be wrung with pity. I was young and strong and handsome with an eagle profile and wavy hair; I was brilliantly clever and I went out to fight your enemies. I endured in the water, I fought the whole sea. I have fought a rock, and gulls and lobsters and seals and a storm. Now I am thin and weak. My joints are like knobs and my limbs like sticks. My face is fallen in with age and my hair is white with salt and suffering. My eyes are dull stones——"

The centre quivered and dwindled. There was another noise beyond the storm and background music and sobbed words from the mouth.

"—my chest is like the ribs of a derelict boat and every breath is an effort——"

The noise was so faint in comparison with the uproar of the wind and rain and waves that it caught and glued attention. The mouth knew this too and tried harder.

"I am going mad. There is lightning playing on the skirts of a wild sea. I am strong again——"

And the mouth sang.

The centre still attended through the singing, the background music, the uproar from outside. The noise came again. The centre could confuse it for a while with thunder.

"Hoé, hoé! Thor's lightning challenges me! Flash after flash, rippling spurts of white fire, bolts flung at Prometheus, blinding white, white, white, searing, the aim of the sky at the man on the rock——"

The noise, if one attended as the centre was forced to attend was dull and distant. It might have been thunder or gun-fire. It might have been the sound of a drum and the mouth seized on that.

"Rata tat tat tat! The soldiers come, my Emperor is taken! Rat a tat!"

It might have been the shifting of furniture in an upper room and the mouth panicked after that thought with the automatic flick of an insect.

"Put it down here. Roll back that corner of the carpet and then you can get the table out. Shall we have it next to the radiogram? Take that record off and put on something rocklike and heroic——"

It might have been flour-sacks slid down an iron ladder to resound on the steel deck.

"Hard a-starboard! Hard a-starboard!"

It might have been the shaking of the copper sheet in the wings.

"I must have the lead or I shall leave the coal flat——"

The cellar door swinging to behind a small child who must go down, down in his sleep to meet the thing he turned from when he was created.

"Off with his head! Down on the block among the kindling and coal-dust!"

But the centre knew. It recognized with a certainity that made the quacking of the mouth no more help than hiccups. The noise was the grating and thump of a spade against an enormous tin box that had been buried.

13

"Mad," said the mouth, "raving mad. I can account for everything, lobsters, maggots, hardness, brilliant reality, the laws of nature, film-trailers, snapshots of sight and sound, flying lizards, enmity—how should a man not be mad? I will tell you what a man is. He goes on four legs till Necessity bends the front end upright and makes a hybrid of him. The finger-prints of those hands are about his spine and just above the rump for proof if you want it. He is a freak, an ejected foetus robbed of his natural development, thrown out in the world with a naked covering of parchment, with too little room for his teeth and a soft bulging skull like a bubble. But nature stirs a pudding there and sets a thunderstorm flickering inside the hardening globe, white, lambent lightning a constant flash and tremble. All your lobsters and film-trailers are nothing but the random intersections of instant bushes of lightning. The sane life of your belly and your cock are on a simple circuit, but how can the stirred pudding keep constant? Tugged at by the pill of the earth, infected by the white stroke that engraved the book, furrowed, lines burned through it by hardship and torment and terror-unbalanced, brain-sick, at your last gasp on a rock in the sea, the pudding has boiled over and you are no worse than raving mad."

Sensations. Coffee. Hock. Gin. Wood. Velvet. Nylon. Mouth. Warm, wet nakedness. Caves, slack like a crevice or tight like the mouth of a red anemone. Full of stings. Domination, identity.

"You are the intersections of all the currents. You do not exist apart from me. If I have gone mad then you have gone mad. You are speaking, in there, you and I are one and mad."

The rock shook and shook again. A sudden coldness struck his face and washed under him.

To be expected.

"Nathaniel!"

Black centre, trying to stir itself like a pudding.

The darkness was shredded by white. He tumbled over among the sensations of the crevice. There was water everywhere and noise and his mouth welcomed both. It spat and coughed. He heaved himself out amid water that swirled to his knees and the wind knocked him down. The trench was like a little sea, like the known and now re-membered extravagances of a returning tide among rocks. What had been a dry trench was half-full of moving water on which streaks of foam were circling and interlacing. The wind was like an express in a tunnel and every-where there was a trickling and washing and pouring.

He scrambled up in the trench, without hearing what his mouth said and suddenly he and his mouth were one.

"You bloody great bully!"

He got his face above the level of the wall and the wind pulled the cheeks in like an airman's. Bird-shot slashed. Then the sky above the old woman jumped. It went white. An instant later the light was switched off and the sky fell on him. He collapsed under the enormous pressure and went down in the water of the trench. The weight withdrew and left him struggling. He got up and the sky fell on him again. This time he was able to lurch along the trench because the weight of water was just not sufficient to break him and the sea in the trench was no higher than his knees. The world came back, storm-grey and torn with flying streamers, and he gave it storm-music, crash of timpany, brass blared and a dazzle of strings. He fought a hero's way from trench to trench through water and music, his clothes shaking and plucked, tattered like the end of a windsock, hands clawing. He and his mouth shouted through the uproar.

"Ajax! Prometheus!"

The old woman was looking down at him as he struggled through bouts of white and dark. Then her head with its silver mask was taken by a whiteness and she hunched against the sky with her headless shoulders. He fell in the white trench over the book with his face against the engraving and the insoluble muck filled his mouth. There came a sudden pressure and silence. He was lifted up and thrown down again, struck against rock. For a moment as the water passed away he saw the Look-out against the sky now empty of the old woman but changed in outline by scattered stones.

"She is loose on the rock. Now she is out of the cellar and in daylight. Hunt her down!"

And the knife was there among all the other sensations, jammed against his ribs. He got it in his hands and pulled the blade open. He began to crawl and hunt and swim from trench to trench. She was leaning over the rail but vanished and he stole after her into the green room. But she was out by the footlights and when he crouched in the wings he saw that he was not dressed properly for the part. His mouth and he were one.

"Change your clothes! Be a naked madman on a rock in the middle of a storm!"

His claws plucked at the tatters and pulled them away. He saw a glimpse of gold braid and an empty seaboot stocking floating away like a handful of waste. He saw a leg, scarred, scaly and stick thin and the music mourned for it.

He remembered the old woman and crawled after her down the High Street to the Red Lion. The back wash of the waves was making a welcome confusion round the three rocks and the confusion hid the place where the red lobster had been. He shouted at the rocks but the old woman would not appear among them. She had slipped away down to the cellar. Then he glimpsed her lying huddled in the crevice and he struggled up to her. He fell on her and began to slash with his knife while his mouth went on shouting.

"That'll teach you to chase me! That'll teach you to chase me out of the cellar through cars and beds and pubs, you at the back and me running, running after my identity disc all the days of my life! Bleed and die."

But he and his voice were one. They knew the blood was sea water and the cold, crumpling flesh that was ripped and torn nothing but oilskin.

Now the voice became a babble, sang, swore, made meaningless syllables, coughed and spat. It filled every tick of time with noise, jammed the sound so that it choked; but the centre began to know itself as other because every instant was not occupied by noise. The mouth spat and deviated into part sense.

"And last of all, hallucination, vision, dream, delusion will haunt you. What else can a madman expect? They will appear to you on the solid rock, the real rock, they will fetter your attention to them and you will be nothing worse than mad."

And immediately the hallucination was there. He knew this before he saw it because there was an awe in the trench, framed by the silent spray that flew over. The hallucination sat on the rock at the end of the trench and at last he faced it through his blurred window. He saw the rest of the trench and crawled along through water that was gravely still unless a gust struck down with a long twitch and shudder of the foamy scum. When he was near, he looked up from the boots, past the knees, to the face and engaged himself to the mouth.

"You are a projection of my mind. But you are a point of attention for me. Stay there."

The lips hardly moved in answer.

"You are a projection of my mind."

He made a snorting sound.

"Infinite regression or better still, round and round the mulberry bush. We could go on like that for ever."

"Have you had enough, Christopher?"

He looked at the lips. They were clear as the words. A tiny shred of spittle joined them near the right corner.

"I could never have invented that."

The eye nearest the Look-out was bloodshot at the outer corner. Behind it or beside it a red strip of sunset ran down out of sight behind the rock. The spray still flew over. You could look at the sunset or the eye but you could not do both. You could not look at the eye and the mouth together. He saw the nose was shiny and leathery brown and full of pores. The left cheek would need a shave soon, for he could see the individual bristles. But he could not look at the whole face together. It was a face that perhaps could be remembered later. It did not move. It merely had this quality of refusing overall inspection. One feature at a time.

"Enough of what?"

"Surviving. Hanging on."

The clothing was difficult to pin down too so that he

had to examine each piece. There was an oilskin—belted, because the buttons had fetched away. There was a woollen pullover inside it, with a roll-neck. The sou'wester was back a little. The hands were resting one on either knee, above the seaboot stockings. Then there were seaboots, good and shiny and wet and solid. They made the rock behind them seem like cardboard, like a painted flat. He bent forward until his bleared window was just above the right instep. There was no background music now and no wind, nothing but black, shiny rubber.

"I hadn't considered."

"Consider now."

"What's the good? I'm mad."

"Even that crevice will crumble."

He tried to laugh up at the bloodshot eye but heard barking noises. He threw words in the face.

"On the sixth day he created God. Therefore I permit you to use nothing but my own vocabulary. In his own image created he Him."

"Consider now."

He saw the eye and the sunset merge. He brought his arms across his face.

"I won't. I can't."

"What do you believe in?"

Down to the black boot, coal black, darkness of the cellar, but now down to a forced answer.

"The thread of my life."

"At all costs."

Repeat after me:

"At all costs."

"So you survived."

"That was luck."

"Inevitability."

"Didn't the others want to live then?"

"There are degrees."

He dropped the curtains of flesh and hair and blotted out the boots. He snarled.

"I have a right to live if I can!"

"Where is that written?"

"Then nothing is written."

"Consider."

He raged on the cardboard rock before the immovable, black feet.

"I will not consider! I have created you and I can create my own heaven."

"You have created it."

He glanced sideways along the twitching water, down at his skeleton legs and knees, felt the rain and spray and the savage cold on his flesh.

He began to mutter.

"I prefer it. You gave me the power to choose and all my life you led me carefully to this suffering because my choice was my own. Oh yes! I understand the pattern. All my life, whatever I had done I should have found myself in the end on that same bridge, at that same time, giving that same order—the right order, the wrong order. Yet, suppose I climbed away from the cellar over the bodies of used and defeated people, broke them to make steps on the road away from you, why should you torture me? If I ate them, who gave me a mouth?"

"There is no answer in your vocabulary."

He squatted back and glared up at the face. He shouted.

"I have considered. I prefer it, pain and all."

"To what?"

He began to rage weakly and strike out at the boots.

"To the black lightning! Go back! Go back!"

He was bruising skin off his hands against the streaming rock. His mouth quacked and he went with it into the last crevice of all.

"Poor mad sailor on a rock!"

He clambered up the High Street.

> *Rage, roar, spout!*
> *Let us have wind, rain, hail, gouts of blood,*
> *Storms and tornadoes . . .*

He ran about on the Look-out, stumbling over scattered stones.

> *. . . hurricanes and typhoons . . .*

There was a half-light, a storm-light. The light was ruled in lines and the sea in ridges and valleys. The monstrous waves were making their way from east to west

211

in an interminable procession and the rock was a trifle among them. But it was charging forward, searing a white way through them, careless of sinking, it was thrusting the Safety Rock forward to burst the ridges like the prow of a ship. It would strike a ridge with the stone prow and burst water into a smother that washed over the fo'c'sle and struck beneath the bridge. Then a storm of shot would sweep over the bridge and strike sense and breath away from his body. He flung himself on a square stone that lay where the old woman had stood with her masked head. He rode it astride, facing into the wind and waves. And again there was background music and a mouth quacking.

"Faster! Faster!"

His rock bored on. He beat it with his heels as if he wore spurs.

"Faster!"

The waves were each an event in itself. A wave would come weltering and swinging in with a storm-light running and flickering along the top like the flicker in a brain. The shallow water beyond the safety rock would occur, so that the nearer part of the wave would rise up, tripped and angry, would roar, swell forward. The Safety Rock would become a pock in a whirlpool of water that spun itself into foam and chewed like a mouth. The whole top of the wave for a hundred yards would move forward and fall into acres of lathering uproar that was launched like an army at the rock.

"Faster!"

His hand found the identity disc and held it out.

The mouth screamed out away from the centre.

"I spit on your compassion!"

There was a recognizable noise away beyond the waves and in the clouds. The noise was not as loud as the sea or the music or the voice but the centre understood. The centre took the body off the slab of rock and bundled it into a trench. As it fell the eye glimpsed a black tendril of lightning that lay across the western sky and the centre screwed down the flaps of flesh and hair. Again there came the sound of the spade against the tin box.

"Hard a-starboard! I'll kill us both, I'll hit the tree with that side and you'll be burst and bitched! There was nothing in writing!"

The centre knew what to do. It was wiser than the mouth. It sent the body scrambling over the rock to the water-hole. It burrowed in among the slime and circling scum. It thrust the hands forward, tore at the water and fell flat in the pool. It wriggled like a seal on a rock with the fresh water streaming out of its mouth. It got at the tamping at the farther end and heaved at the stones. There was a scraping and breaking sound and then the cascade of falling stones and water. There was a wide space of storm-light, waves. There was a body lying in the slimy hollow where the fresh water had been.

"Mad! Proof of madness!"

It made the body wriggle back out of the hole, sent it

up to the place where the Look-out had been.

There were branches of the black lightning over the sky, there were noises. One branch ran down into the sea, through the great waves, petered out. It remained there. The sea stopped moving, froze, became paper, painted paper that was torn by a black line. The rock was painted on the same paper. The whole of the painted sea was tilted but nothing ran downhill into the black crack which had opened in it. The crack was utter, was absolute, was three times real.

The centre did not know if it had flung the body down or if it had turned the world over. There was rock before its face and it struck with lobster claws that sank in. It watched the rock between the claws.

The absolute lightning spread. There was no noise now because noise had become irrelevant. There was no music, no sound from the tilted, motionless sea.

The mouth quacked on for a while then dribbled into silence.

There was no mouth.

Still the centre resisted. It made the lightning do its work according to the laws of this heaven. It perceived in some mode of sight without eyes that pieces of the sky between the branches of black lightning were replaced by pits of nothing. This made the fear of the centre, the rage of the centre vomit in a mode that required no mouth. It screamed into the pit of nothing voicelessly, wordlessly.

"I shit on your heaven!"

The lines and tendrils felt forward through the sea. A segment of storm dropped out like a dead leaf and there was a gap that joined sea and sky through the horizon. Now the lightning found reptiles floating and flying motionlessly and a tendril ran to each. The reptiles resisted, changing shape a little, then they too, dropped out and were gone. A valley of nothing opened up through Safety Rock.

The centre attended to the rock between its claws. The rock was harder than rock, brighter, firmer. It hurt the serrations of the claws that gripped.

The sea twisted and disappeared. The fragments were not visible going away, they went into themselves, dried up, destroyed, erased like an error.

The lines of absolute blackness felt forward into the rock and it was proved to be as insubstantial as the painted water. Pieces went and there was no more than an island of papery stuff round the claws and everywhere else there was the mode that the centre knew as nothing.

The rock between the claws was solid. It was square and there was an engraving on the surface. The black lines sank in, went through and joined.

The rock between the claws was gone.

There was nothing but the centre and the claws. They were huge and strong and inflamed to red. They closed on each other. They contracted. They were outlined like a night sign against the absolute nothingness and they gripped their whole strength into each other.

The serrations of the claws broke. They were lambent and real and locked.

The lightning crept in. The centre was unaware of anything but the claws and the threat. It focused its awareness on the crumbled serrations and the blazing red. The lightning came forward. Some of the lines pointed to the centre, waiting for the moment when they could pierce it. Others lay against the claws, playing over them, prying for a weakness, wearing them away in a compassion that was timeless and without mercy.

14

The jetty, if the word would do for a long pile of boulders, was almost under the tide at the full. The drifter came in towards it, engine stopped, with the last of her way and the urging of the west wind. There was a wintry sunset behind her so that to the eyes on the beach she seemed soon a black shape from which the colour had all run away and been stirred into the low clouds that hung just above the horizon. There was a leaden tinge to the water except in the path of the drifter—a brighter valley of red and rose and black that led back to the dazzling horizon under the sun.

The watcher on the beach did not move. He stood, his seaboots set in the troughs of dry sand that his last steps had made, and waited. There was a cottage at his back and then the slow slope of the island.

The telegraph rang astern in the drifter and she checked her way with a sudden swirl of brighter water from the screws. A fender groaned against stone. Two men jumped on to the jetty and sought about them for the bollards that were not there. An arm gesticulated from the wheel-house. The men caught their ropes round boulders and stood, holding on.

An officer stepped on to the jetty, came quickly towards the beach and jumped down to the dry sand. The wind ruffled papers that he held in his hand so that they chattered like the dusty leaves of late summer. But here they were the only leaves. There was sand, a cottage, rocks and the sea. The officer laboured along in the dry sand with his papers chattering and came to a halt a yard from the watcher.

"Mr. Campbell?"

"Aye. You'll be from the mainland about the————?"

"That's right."

Mr. Campbell removed his cloth cap and put it back again.

"You've not been over-quick."

The officer looked at him solemnly.

"My name's Davidson, by the way. Over-quick. Do you know, Mr. Campbell, that I do this job, seven days a week?"

Mr. Campbell moved his seaboots suddenly. He peered forward into Davidson's grey and lined face. There was a faint, sweet smell on the breath and the eyes that did not blink were just a fraction too wide open.

Mr. Campbell took off his cap and put it on again.

"Well now. Fancy that!"

The lower part of Davidson's face altered to the beginnings of a grin without humour.

"It's quite a widespread war, you know."

Mr. Campbell nodded slowly.

"I'm sorry that I spoke. A sad harvest for you, Captain. I do not know how you can endure it."

The grin disappeared.

"I wouldn't change."

Mr. Campbell tilted his head sideways and peered into Davidson's face.

"No? I beg your pardon, sir. Come now and see where we found it."

He turned and laboured away along the sand. He stopped and pointed down to where an arm of water was confined by a shingly spit.

"It was there, still held by the lifebelt. You'll see, of course. There was a broken orange-box and a tin. And the lineweed. When we have a nor'wester the lineweed gets caught there—and anything else that's floating."

Davidson looked sideways at him.

"It seems important to you, Mr. Campbell, but what I really want is the identity disc. Did you remove that from the body?"

"No. No. I touched—as little as possible."

"A brown disc about the size of a penny, probably worn round the neck?"

"No. I touched nothing."

Davidson's face set grim again.

"One can always hope, I suppose."

Mr. Campbell clasped his hands, rubbed them restlessly,

cleared his throat.

"You'll take it away tonight?"

Now Davidson peered in his turn.

"Dreams?"

Mr. Campbell looked away at the water. He muttered.

"The wife——"

He glanced up at the too-wide eyes, the face that seemed to know more than it could bear. He no longer evaded the meeting but shrank a little and answered with sudden humility.

"Aye."

Davidson nodded, slowly.

Now two ratings were standing on the beach before the cottage. They bore a stretcher.

Mr. Campbell pointed.

"It is in the lean-to by the house, sir. I hope there is as little to offend you as possible. We used paraffin."

"Thank you."

Davidson toiled back along the beach and Mr. Campbell followed him. Presently they stopped. Davidson turned and looked down.

"Well——"

He put his hand to the breast pocket of his battledress and brought out a flat bottle. He looked Mr. Campbell in the eye, grinned with the lower part of his face, pulled out the cork and swigged, head back. The ratings watched him without comment.

"Here goes, then."

Davidson went to the lean-to, taking a torch from his trouser pocket. He ducked through the broken door and disappeared.

The ratings stood without movement. Mr. Campbell waited, silently, and contemplated the lean-to as though he were seeing it for the first time. He surveyed the mossed stones, the caved-in and lichenous roof as though they were a profound and natural language that men were privileged to read only on a unique occasion.

There was no noise from inside.

Even on the drifter there was no conversation. The only noises were the sounds of the water falling over on the little beach.

Hush. Hush.

The sun was a half-circle in a bed of crimson and slate.

Davidson came out again. He carried a small disc, swinging from a double string. His right hand went to the breast pocket. He nodded to the ratings.

"Go on, then."

Mr. Campbell watched Davidson fumble among his papers. He saw him examining the disc, peering close, transferring details carefully to a file. He saw him put the disc away, crouch, rub his hands backwards and forwards in the dry, clean sand. Mr. Campbell spread his arms wide in a gesture of impotence and dropped them.

"I do not know, sir. I am older than you but I do not know."

Davidson said nothing. He stood up again and took out

his bottle.

"Don't you have second sight up here?"

Mr. Campbell looked unhappily at the lean-to.

"Don't joke, sir. That was unworthy of you."

Davidson came down from his swig. Two faces approached each other. Campbell read the face line by line as he had read the lean-to. He flinched from it again and looked away at the place where the sun was going down—seemingly for ever.

The ratings came out of the lean-to. They carried a stretcher between them that was no longer empty.

"All right, lads. There's a tot waiting for you. Carry on."

The two sailors went cautiously away through the sand towards the jetty. Davidson turned to Mr. Campbell.

"I have to thank you, Mr. Campbell, in the name of this poor officer."

Mr. Campbell took his eyes away from the stretcher.

"They are wicked things, those lifebelts. They give a man hope when there is no longer any call for it. They are cruel. You do not have to thank me, Mr. Davidson."

He looked at Davidson in the gloom, carefully, eye to eye. Davidson nodded.

"Maybe. But I thank you."

"I did nothing."

The two men turned and watched the ratings lifting the stretcher to the low jetty.

"And you do this every day."

"Every day."

"Mr. Davidson——"

Mr. Campbell paused so that Davidson turned towards him again. Mr. Campbell did not immediately meet his eye.

"——we are the type of human intercourse. We meet here, apparently by chance, a meeting unpredictable and never to be repeated. Therefore I should like to ask you a question with perhaps a brutal answer."

Davidson pushed his cap back on his head and frowned. Mr. Campbell looked at the lean-to.

"Broken, defiled. Returning to the earth, the rafters rotted, the roof fallen in——a wreck. Would you believe that anything ever lived there?"

Now the frown was bewildered.

"I simply don't follow you, I'm afraid."

"All those poor people——"

"The men I——?"

"The harvest. The sad harvest. You know nothing of my——shall I say——official beliefs, Mr. Davidson; but living for all these days next to that poor derelict——Mr. Davidson. Would you say there was any——surviving? Or is that all? Like the lean-to?"

"If you're worried about Martin——whether he suffered or not——"

They paused for a while. Beyond the drifter the sun sank like a burning ship, went down, left nothing for a reminder but clouds like smoke.

Mr. Campbell sighed.

"Aye," he said, "I meant just that."

"Then don't worry about him. You saw the body. He didn't even have time to kick off his seaboots."

Afterword by Philippa Gregory

This is an afterword, rather than a foreword, because any study of this extraordinary novel has to consider the ending: the most important section in this novel. Read at their simplest, the final pages are a 'twist in the tail' like the playful reverse of a traditional short story, but these pages are far more than this: they are a shocking revelation to the reader that the whole novel has been an illusion of the narrator Pincher Martin. In place of the illusion we suddenly see a snapshot of the real world, and a suggestion of what has really taken place.

The 'twist' is the total inversion of the story. We readers thought that we were reading a story about survival, in which the survival of the material world, of the mind and body of a profoundly materialistic man whose very nickname, 'Pincher', implies grabbing, is the drama and chief concern. It seems to be a novel rather like one of the earliest novels ever written: *Robinson Crusoe* – a novel about marooning and survival. Shockingly, in the last pages we learn in a few brutal phrases that the story was not, as we thought, about life, but was all along about dying a death so

225

fast that the narrator did not even have time to kick off his seaboots and swim, but was dragged down to drown, and the story which we have followed was nothing more than his last anguished thoughts, as drowning men are said to have.

This is much more profound and thought-provoking than a mere 'twist in the tail' trick. It means that we the reader have been like Pincher, fretting about water and anemones, rocks, seals and seagulls, and it has all been the last illusion of a dying consciousness. Our reading experience is further devalued because Pincher slowly reveals himself as a wicked man – a rapist and a murderer. This novel, on which we have spent some hours of our time, is the final misunderstanding of a man who has made many mistakes. Not until the very last moment does he begin to learn – the turbulent condition of the island is the turmoil of his drowning, but he never knows this, just as he never knows his own nature, his love for Nat, the beauty of Mary, or the wisdom that Nat would have volunteered. It is only at the moment of his death that he sees truly at last – and all he sees, all he can see, is a dark lightning.

Our reading experience of this novel makes us reflect on reading in general. In all novels the narrator persuades us of a reality and we volunteer to be drawn in. Golding exposes the whole complicit delusion of reading any novel when the Pincher Martin narrator, that we have believed and trusted, turns out to have been dead all along. With the outstanding confidence of a great novelist, Golding

226

at once sets another scene: another island, another naval crew, which we are again supposed to read as a reality. Some parts of this new story are told in conversation, but overall the story is described by an omniscient narrator who – once again – we trust. It is no accident that the last lines of dialogue, the only 'live' dialogue of the novel, are a misunderstanding, when Mr Campbell asks the officer Mr Davidson if there is any sort of afterlife, if the corpse had 'lived' among the decay of the lean-to; and the naval officer replies that the death was too quick for suffering. In this layered world that Golding has created, there are illusions and misunderstandings, but nothing is certain.

Nothing is certain and nothing is clear! I love this novel dearly; but it has puzzled many readers, and there was much that I did not understand at a first reading, nor still now after many re-readings. I confess too that I had to read criticism of the book to learn that the island with its meticulous description of the detail is Pincher's own mouth, his missing tooth. His egoism is such that when he is trying to imagine his survival, he imagines his own body; his illusions are random facts that he can remember. This is not an easy book to read in any way, not for comprehension, not for entertainment.

So why do I like it so much? Firstly, I think this is a novel by an author at the peak of his ability, uncompromising in the pursuit of the story he wants to tell. It is absolutely convincing even when it is describing the wildest of delusions. The collapse of Pincher's consciousness is meticulously mapped. It would be hard to imagine a more powerful study of a single mind under pressure. The terror of madness is always a powerful motif in a novel, since the novel itself is a sort of madness: the reader enters into an imaginary world and experiences profound emotions about things that are not real. Many novels that describe a narrator's slide into madness do so by studying an individual entrapped by intensely described others. But in this novel there are very few characters at all, and they are seen only and exclusively through the darkness of Pincher's vision, they are symptoms more than characters. Mary, the woman he desires, is viciously caricatured and her struggle against his assault shown in the most unsympathetic light. The friend that he deeply loves, Nat, is introduced to the reader as a fool, described as an insect. In one of the rare honest declarations, Pincher knows that he loves and hates Nat.

Many readers find Pincher easy to dislike, and it is a triumph by the author to have us stay in the company of a hateful and untrustworthy narrator. Only in his descriptions of his childhood is he a sympathetic character. He is never clear about his suffering at the hands of his mother, but Golding tells us enough to suggest that the dangerous man was a damaged child. Only at the end of the novel, as a vital part of the inversion of the story, does Golding show us Christopher Martin – as his identity disc names him – not Pincher, of the greedy claw hands. We see Christopher as a body worth recovering, not a murderer marooned on a barren rock. We see the

228

young man who gave his life for his country and not the actor who tried to cheat his way out of service, and we see other men also damaged by war: the naval officer who does his work with the help of drink, his men who are promised a measure of rum for carrying the corpse, and the crofter who has had nightmares since the body was washed ashore.

The end of the novel offers us a hard spiritual truth. Mr Campbell asks if there is any 'surviving' – he seems to mean is Christopher Martin as dead and decaying as his last home, the collapsing lean-to? Mr Davidson answers in terms of suffering and says that the death was so quick that Christopher Martin drowned before he could kick off his boots. We the reader, know better. We know that in those seconds there was great suffering, a suffering that seemed to Christopher to go on for days, in which he reviewed his life and understood some of it. His last moments as he realized that the dark lightning that had come for him, was Nat's earlier description of heaven:

Take us as we are now and heaven would be sheer negation . . . A sort of black lightning destroying everything that we call life.

What Nat describes is not easy to understand, but it is – as he says – what heaven must be for sinners. Martin cannot see heaven, but he can see a compassionate end to the terrible ego that is himself. Martin knew at the end that

though he hated Nat, he loved him too, and his final vision
was that the dark lightning had come for him 'in a compassion that was timeless and without mercy'.

The novels of William Golding

ff

Lord of the Flies

A plane crashes on a desert island and the only survivors, a group of schoolboys, assemble on the beach and wait to be rescued. By day they inhabit a land of bright fantastic birds and dark blue seas, but at night their dreams are haunted by the image of a terrifying beast. As the boys' delicate sense of order fades, so their childish dreams are transformed into something more primitive, and their behaviour starts to take on a murderous, savage significance.

ff

The Inheritors

This was a different voice; not the voice of the people.
It was the voice of other.

When the spring came the people moved back to their familiar home. But this year strange things were happening – inexplicable sounds and smells; unexpected acts of violence; and new, unimaginable creatures half glimpsed through the leaves. Seen through the eyes of a small tribe of Neanderthals whose world is hanging in the balance, *The Inheritors* explores the emergence of a new race, *Homo sapiens*, whose growing dominance threatens an entire way of life.

ff

Free Fall

Somehow, somewhere, Sammy Mountjoy lost his freedom, the faculty of freewill 'that cannot be debated but only experienced, like a colour or the taste of potatoes'. As he retraces his life in an effort to discover why he no longer has the power to choose and decide for himself, the narrative moves between England and a prisoner-of-war camp in Germany. In *Free Fall*, his fourth novel, William Golding has created a poetic fiction, and an allegory, as moving as it is unforgettable.

ff

The Spire

Dean Jocelin has a vision: that God has chosen him to erect a great spire on his cathedral. His mason anxiously advises against it, for the old cathedral was built without foundations. Nevertheless, the spire rises octagon upon octagon, pinnacle by pinnacle, until the stone pillars shriek and the ground beneath it swims. Its shadow falls ever darker on the world below, and on Dean Jocelin in particular.

ff

The Pyramid

Oliver is eighteen, and wants to enjoy himself before going to university. But this is the 1920s, and he lives in Stilbourne, a small English country town, where everyone knows what everyone else is getting up to, and where love, lust and rebellion are closely followed by revenge and embarrassment. Written with great perception and subtlety, *The Pyramid* is William Golding's funniest and most light-hearted novel, which probes the painful awkwardness of the late teens, the tragedy and farce of life in a small community and the consoling power of music.

ff

The Scorpion God

Three short novels show Golding at his subtle, ironic, mysterious best. In *The Scorpion God* we see the world of ancient Egypt at the time of the earliest pharaohs. *Clonk Clonk* is a graphic account of a crippled youth's triumph over his tormentors in a primitive matriarchal society. And *Envoy Extraordinary* is a tale of Imperial Rome where the emperor loves his illegitimate grandson more than his own arrogant, loutish heir.

ff

Darkness Visible

Darkness Visible opens at the height of the London Blitz, when a naked child steps out of an all-consuming fire. Miraculously saved but hideously scarred, soon tormented at school and at work, Matty becomes a wanderer, a seeker after some unknown redemption. Two more lost children await him, twins as exquisite as they are loveless. Toni dabbles in political violence; Sophy, in sexual tyranny. As Golding weaves their destinies together, his book reveals both the inner and outer darkness of our world.

ff

The Paper Men

Fame, success, fortune, a drink problem slipping over the edge into alcoholism, a dead marriage, the incurable itches of middle-aged lust. For Wilfred Barclay, novelist, the final unbearable irritation is Professor Rick L. Tucker, implacable in his determination to become The Barclay Man. Locked in a lethal relationship they stumble across Europe, shedding wives, self-respect and illusions. The climax of their odyssey, when it comes, is as inevitable as it is unexpected.

ff

The Double Tongue

Golding's final novel, left in draft at his death, tells the story of a priestess of Apollo. Arieka is one of the last to prophesy at Delphi, in the shadowy years when the Romans were securing their grip on the tribes and cities of Greece. The plain, unloved daughter of a local grandee, she is rescued from the contempt and neglect of her family by her Delphic role. Her ambiguous attitude to the god and her belief in him seem to move in parallel with the decline of the god himself – but things are more complicated than they appear.

ff

Rites of Passage

Sailing to Australia in the early years of the nineteenth century, Edmund Talbot keeps a journal to amuse his godfather back in England. Full of wit and disdain, he records the mounting tensions on the ancient, sinking warship where officers, sailors, soldiers and emigrants jostle in the cramped spaces below decks. Then a single passenger, the obsequious Reverend Colley, attracts the animosity of the sailors, and in the seclusion of the fo'castle something happens to bring him into a 'hell of degradation', where shame is a force deadlier than the sea itself.

ff

Close Quarters

In a wilderness of heat, stillness and sea mists, a ball is held on a ship becalmed halfway to Australia. In this surreal, fête-like atmosphere the passengers dance and flirt, while beneath them thickets of weed like green hair spread over the hull. The sequel to *Rites of Passage*, *Close Quarters*, the second volume in Golding's acclaimed sea trilogy, is imbued with his extraordinary sense of menace. Half-mad with fear, with drink, with love and opium, everyone on this leaky, unsound hulk is 'going to pieces'. And in a nightmarish climax the very planks seem to twist themselves alive as the ship begins to come apart at the seams.

ff

Fire Down Below

The third volume of William Golding's acclaimed sea trilogy. A decrepit warship sails on the last stretch of its voyage to Sydney Cove. It has been blown off course and battered by wind, storm and ice. Nothing but rope holds the disintegrating hull together. And after a risky operation to reset its foremast with red-hot metal, an unseen fire begins to smoulder below decks.